GRAYSEN FOXX
and the Curse of the Illuminerdy

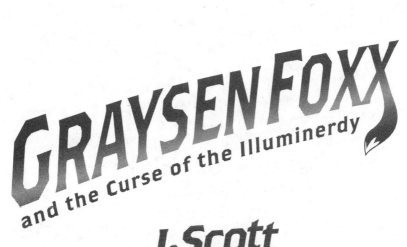

GRAYSEN FOXX

and the Curse of the Illuminerdy

J. Scott Savage

Illustrations by Brandon Dorman

SHADOW
MOUNTAIN
PUBLISHING

To Lisa Greene and Barbara Apsley,
who instill a love of reading and a desire to learn
and explore in elementary school kids who need
their support and encouragement so much.

© 2024 J. Scott Savage
Illustrations © 2024 Brandon Dorman

Visit us at shadowmountain.com

Library of Congress Cataloging-in-Publication Data

(CIP data on file)

ISBN 978-1-63993-170-5

Printed in the United States of America

1 2 3 4 5 LBC 27 26 25 24 23

CHAPTER 1
Who's Afraid?

Disguises come in all shapes and sizes. Some are on the outside, like the costumes kids would be wearing in a couple of weeks for the school Halloween parade. Others are on the inside, like the head of Ordinary Elementary, Principal Luna, who pretended to be an iron-fisted tyrant when she was really an experienced treasure hunter eagerly awaiting the next adventure, just like me.

Then there are the disguises so cleverly con-ceived, so deviously deceptive, so carefully concealed that you don't even realize there is anything hidden behind them until it smashes some poor sap in the nose like a perfectly aimed dodgeball—turning their school days upside down and filling their nights with the twisted dreams of a tormented fifth grader.

I am Graysen Foxx, finder of secrets, solver of mysteries, explorer of the unknown—and also the sap in this story.

1

The kid who clued me in to the area under the stage was Jake Campbell, although most kids just called him "Toes" on account his abnormally large feet and how he tended to take off his shoes in class.

Along with his sizeable sneakers, Toes was known for being in nineteen plays, fourteen holiday pageants, eleven musical numbers, seven talent shows, and the bathroom safety skit Mr. Flickersnicker, the janitor, made us watch after the McNaughton twins tried to see how many pencils they could flush down the toilet at once.

According to Toes, the enormous cobweb-filled shadow world the drama kids called *Wardrobe* contained every costume used in every play since Ordinary Elementary opened nearly a hundred years ago. That fact alone made my archaeologist senses tingle like the time in science class we rubbed our hair with balloons to learn about static electricity. But the treasure I was searching for that morning wasn't a costume at all.

Maya and Jack Delgado, my two best friends and third-grade treasure hunters in training, wanted to win the pizza party promised to the classroom with the best Halloween decorations. According to Toes, under the stage was an old painting so spooky it would guarantee that the classroom hanging it on their wall would take first place. As a reward for helping me recover Principal Redbeard's Treasure a few weeks ago—and because they were such good friends—I'd agreed to help the twins find it.

So there we were, exploring our way through decades of dusty dance slippers and mountains of moldy masks.

Maya poked through a rack of ball gowns to my left while Jack, her elusive twin, kept watch near the door. The area was off limits to kids who weren't in drama, and none of us were actors.

"I don't get why princesses always wear these floofy dresses," Maya said, pushing aside a yellow satin gown with enough lace to provide the entire kindergarten with snowflake-making material for a month.

"Maybe they just want to look nice?" I climbed a stool to peek over a stack of hatboxes. The only thing there was a sequined white glove circa the mid-1980s covered in spider-webs. A long-legged spider glared at me with what looked like at least a dozen angry eyes, and I jerked backward, knocking over the stool and tumbling to the splintery wood floor with a thump.

Maya looked over. "Nice fall."

"It wasn't a fall," I said, getting up. "It was a strategic retreat from a vicious arachnid that could probably have killed me with one touch of its sharp fangs."

She smirked and said under her breath, "Most spiders aren't venomous."

Trying to change the subject, I examined one of the gowns. "It's pretty."

"But totally impractical." Maya shoved the dress back in place. "The first time a princess has to crawl through a secret passage or fight an assassin, that material is going to catch on every sharp corner in the castle."

"I don't remember princesses needing to fight assassins very often," I said.

She snorted and squeezed around a set of armor made of soup cans and foil. "That's because no one tells the stories right. Aurora poked her finger on a spinning wheel, but she was actually looking for a battle axe to fight Maleficent. Mulan wiped out an entire Hun army single-handedly. And Cinderella only pretended to mop the floors and clean out the fireplaces when she was really gathering info to take down her vicious stepmother and creepy stepsisters the first chance she got. Rags make fantastic espionage clothes."

I had no idea.

"Speaking of espionage," she whispered. "Are you sure no one followed us here? Lizzy Stonebrook says her spies haven't spotted any suspicious activity, and ever since Cameron and the first graders embarrassed the Doodler, he's been holed up in his office drawing pictures of angry kittens. But Raven's been too quiet lately."

Raven Ransom, aka Red Raven, had been my arch-nemesis for as long as I could remember—figuring out what I was hunting for, then cutting in at the last minute to swoop my find away.

During the search for the treasure of Principal Redbeard, she'd used every dirty trick in the book to reach it before me, including bribing the Second-Grade Spy Network, distracting me with student emergencies, and convincing the Doodler—boss of the Venerable but Quick-Tempered Order of the Sixth Graders—that I'd betrayed him.

In the end we'd been forced to work together, combining her intelligence and cunning with my investigation and puzzle-solving skills to thwart our real enemy and rescue Redbeard's stash of toys. "I really think she's turned her powers to good," I said. "Sometimes all it takes is—"

"Shh," Maya said, pointing to where something was jangling the metal hangers like a librarian searching for her favorite cardigan. A shadowy figure pushed its way clumsily through the rows of costumes a few feet away. "I bet it's Rotten Raven, back up to her old tricks."

I shook my head. "Raven would never be that obvious." And she definitely wouldn't have made the low half cry, half howl sound that came from the direction of the movement.

"That sounds like a ghost," Maya whispered, ducking behind the armor. "You didn't say anything about this place being haunted."

"I d-didn't know it was," I stuttered.

But that wasn't entirely true. Stories of spirits haunting the theater had been around long before I started school. Kids who didn't get parts they wanted. Actors whose overly dramatic death scenes went on way too long. Angry parents who weren't allowed to take pictures or use their cell phones during the show.

Even Toes had seen them—he claimed the ghost of Ordinary Elementary's first drama teacher, Agnes Fishbottom, once threw a shoe at him for getting his lines wrong during a dress rehearsal of *A Christmas Carol.*

Pointed ears and shaggy brown fur appeared above a rack of kindergarten-sized Oompa Loompa suits as the creature moved closer.

"That's no spirit," Maya squeaked, her dark eyes growing round.

But what was it? I'd seen some enormous rats inside the Maze of Death below the school, and only the timely kazoo playing of the second-grade spies had kept me, Jack, and Maya from being captured by the mutant chamelepigs in the Forsaken Field, but this looked way bigger than either of those.

Grabbing Maya's hand, I yanked her back toward the stage entrance. "Let's get out of here."

At the sound of my voice, a giant wolf standing upright on its back legs lurched into the open—at least six feet tall with a pointed snout, sharp fangs, and fiery orange eyes.

I elbowed my way past a rack of zebra outfits as Maya and I raced down a row of Lion King costumes. But the monster hunting us was too fast. With a ferocious growl, it knocked over a stack of plastic flamingos and leaped in front of us, cutting off our escape.

"This way," Maya said, turning toward the back of the costume storage.

The monster was incredibly fast for its size. Its paws thumped across the floor, its crying howl growing louder with every step.

With the fanged horror only feet behind, Maya and I ran straight into a brick wall.

It was the end of the line, and maybe the end of our lives.

Was this it? In this musical we call life, would I finish my treasure hunting days buried beneath a stack of stinky wool coats last worn by awkward elementary school dancers in *Fiddler on the Roof*?

Turning slowly around, I looked up into the eyes of the ferocious beast. Globes of white foam dripped from its hungry jaws onto the floor as it let out a frenzied howl.

In an act of pure desperation, Maya grabbed a jeweled tiara from a nearby mannequin head, wound up, and punched it into the beast's stomach.

Yelping, the wolf backed away.

She smacked it again, bending the tiara nearly in half as the wolf cried out, raising its paws to protect itself.

Apparently some princess clothes did come in handy in a battle.

Maya raised the mangled crown, and the wolf shook its massive head. "Stop it. That hurts."

Looking closer, I could just make out a second pair

of eyes watching me—not from the wolf's face but from behind the matted brown fur halfway down its body. As I leaned toward them, the eyes blinked.

"Jack?"

CHAPTER 2
An Unexpected Treasure

Elementary school is like a 64 pack of Crayola Crayons. Sometimes you break your forest green in the middle of a picture only to discover that shamrock is what you really needed all along.

Maya peered at her twin. "What are you doing in there?"

"I thought it would be awesome for Halloween," Jack said, his voice muted by the fur of the Big Bad Wolf costume.

I touched a piece of the "foam" leaking from the wolf's mouth and discovered it was Styrofoam balls used to fill the snout. "Why were you howling?"

From inside the costume that was a good three feet taller than him, Jack shook his head.

"I wasn't howling. I was yelling." He shifted from one foot to the other. "The zipper's stuck and I have to go to the bathroom."

Around school, Jack was known as "The Ghost" because he was so fast and quiet he could slip in and out of any classroom without being noticed. Also like a ghost, he didn't like to talk when he was being watched and would only speak out loud when he was in the dark—or apparently inside a wolf. The rest of the time, he relied on whispering to his sister. The price of working in the shadows.

"You were supposed to be keeping an eye on the door," I said as Maya turned Jack around and pulled at the zipper on the back of the costume.

"Sorry." The wolf shrugged. "I got bored."

"Stop moving," Maya said. She tugged on the zipper again, but it wouldn't budge. "I think it's caught on the fur."

Jack crossed his legs.

The key to any good treasure hunt is discipline, and the kid could have blown the whole operation by leaving his post. To be fair, the first rule of treasure hunting is that nothing goes exactly the way you planned. But the second rule is to always go to the bathroom before an expedition, which it looked like we needed to revisit.

Still, we had bigger fish to fry. By the way he was shifting from one foot to the other, it was clear that if we didn't get Jack out of that costume soon, I would have some major explaining to do to Toes—and the drama teacher.

Looking for something to help unstick the wolf costume, I pushed aside a stack of boxes and gasped.

Maya grinned. "More spiders?"

"No, look," I whispered, pointing at the framed canvas leaning against the wall. "It's the painting."

According to legend, the year Ordinary Elementary

was built, a wealthy donor contrib-
uted more than a million dollars to its construction. As a
reward for his generous gift,
the school hung an oil painting of him just inside the front
doors.

But students and teachers
soon began complaining that
the portrait made them uneasy.
One glance at the figure on the
dusty canvas made it easy to
understand why.

Standing in front of the
doors to the newly built school,
the old man glared angrily out
from the frame like someone had just eaten his last piece of
Halloween candy. I hadn't seen a face that grim since the
Turkleson sisters accidentally glued their mouths shut while
making papier-mâché globes.

Over pinched lips and a nose as thin and straight as
the edge of a ruler, the portrait's cold gray eyes stared right
through me.

"He looks like he has a mouth full of sour gummy
worms," Maya said.

"Or grave dirt," I added with a shiver. This was going
to win the best-decorated-classroom contest for sure. I just
hoped it wouldn't give the kids who saw it nightmares.

Maya reached for the painting, but I held out my hand.

"This is a historical artifact. We have to make a record of everything we find." I took out my field journal, noting the relic's size, condition, and location. The frame was solid oak carved with a pattern of raised and lowered rectangles.

Even though the canvas was old, the man's eyes seemed alive, watching every move I made. I tried stepping to one side, but the eyes followed me no matter where I went.

Once I was done with my notes, I nodded for Maya to take the painting.

"Heavy," she said, hoisting the portrait before handing it to Jack, who was holding out his hairy paws. "How do you think it ended up here?"

I shook my head. "I only know that after enough people complained about the painting, it was moved to the library. Then the art room. After that, the records are sketchy. Some people say it was stored with the piles of test results students have to take every year. Others say it was sold—or burned."

"Maybe someone brought it here to be used as a prop," Maya said as Jack—no longer wearing the wolf outfit— appeared to our right.

"How did you get over there?" I asked.

Jack whispered to his sister.

"He says he just came back from going to the bath-room."

"But how did you get out of the costume?" I asked.

Jack whispered again and Maya shook her head. "No I didn't. The zipper was stuck."

She looked at me. "Did *you* help Jack?"

"Of course not. I was busy examining the—" I looked around. "Where's the painting?"

Maya turned to Jack. "Where did you put it?"

Jack shrugged and whispered.

"Yes, you did," Maya said. "I handed it to you just a minute ago."

Jack whispered so forcefully I could almost make out a couple of his words. They didn't sound happy.

Maya ran her fingers through her dark hair. "He swears I unzipped his costume and he's been in the bathroom until just now. But that's impossible."

"Unless—" Tugging down my fedora, I peered into the passageway and spotted a hastily dropped wolf costume. "Did you see who unstuck the zipper?"

Jack shook his head, crossed his legs, and pantomimed running. He'd been too busy hurrying to the bathroom to look around.

The clues to the mystery came together faster than a two-piece Lego set.

"Someone must have followed us under the stage when Jack was trying on the wolf costume," I said. "They came up behind us while we were looking at the painting, loosened the zipper on Jack's costume, then ducked out of sight while he took it off. As soon as he was gone, they dressed up as the wolf, took the painting from you, then changed out of the costume and escaped before Jack returned."

It was a plan as brilliantly daring as it was evil.

13

"Look," Maya said, spotting a metallic gleam next to the wolf costume. She pushed aside the fur and picked up a multipurpose tool that could be used as a screwdriver, knife, saw, and several other tools—including pliers. Whoever stole the painting must have left the tool behind in their hurry to escape before we noticed them.

Maya turned the tool over, revealing a pair of engraved initials. *R.R.* "Raven!" she snarled.

Jack raced toward the door, but I called him back. "Don't bother," I said. "By now she's probably hanging the painting on the wall of her classroom."

"She'll win the contest for sure," Maya said.

Jack shuffled toward her and tilted his head.

Maya snorted. "No, I don't think she'll share her pizza with you."

So much for my archnemesis using her powers for good.

Shrugging, Jack pointed back to the soup-can armor we'd passed earlier.

"It *is* creepy," Maya admitted. "But not half as spooky as the painting. You should have seen the old man's eyes."

I stared at the spot where the portrait had been only a few minutes earlier, feeling as bitter as the cafeteria's baked brussels sprout goulash. Maya had warned me about Raven, and I hadn't listened. I really thought she had changed.

"Let's get out of here," I said. "School starts in half an hour, and no doubt Raven will rub our noses in her success all day."

I kicked the wall, wishing I didn't have such a trusting nature, and something moved.

Leaning down for a closer look, I noticed that one of the bricks had slid slightly out from the others. Was it just loose mortar—or something else? The building was old, but the wall didn't seem to be crumbling and none of the other bricks looked loose.

When I tugged the brick, it slid out, exposing a small compartment. I reached inside, my hand closing around a tarnished metal star. It looked like the kind of thing someone would get for winning a race. On the front of the star was a picture of a bumblebee and the words "First Place, 1927"—the year the school opened.

I flipped it over. On the back, someone had scratched an image I'd never seen before. It looked like the plastic protractors we used in math with an eye in the middle and seven stars along the curve of the top.

Something was written underneath, but I didn't recognize the symbols.

"What is that?" Maya asked.

"Not sure," I murmured. "But I think we might have just found something way more valuable than free pizza."

CHAPTER 3
You Can't Book This

There are three things you don't mess with in this world: another kid's cubby, a parent's pick-up routine, and a book from the library.

As soon as the lunch bell rang, Maya, Jack, and I headed straight for the library—the home of knowledge, really funny books, and the fastest school librarian west of the Mississippi. We were here for the former—and the latter.

The minute I stepped up to the library counter, Mrs. Hall slapped down a double stack of *Dog Mans*—my latest read of choice—and a clean bookmark.

The librarian was a peach, but I shook my head.

"I'm not here for books today."

She frowned. "You aren't feeling sick, are you? I hear there's a nasty stomach virus going around."

I looked over my shoulder to make sure no one was watching. "It's not that."

"Ahh." She nodded covertly and dropped me a wink. "Another hunt," she said in a soft voice.

"How did you know?" Maya asked.

"I'd recognize that look anywhere," Mrs. Hall said. "I imagine it's how Sherlock Holmes must have looked when Dr. Mortimer told him and Dr. Watson about the demonic hound haunting the mires of Dartmoor."

I didn't know anything about demonic hounds, but they sounded interesting.

"What can I help you with?" the librarian continued.

Jack opened one of the *Dog Man* books and immediately began chuckling as I slid the medal across the counter. "Ever seen anything like this?"

"Hmm, it's a little before my time," she said, putting on her reading glasses. "But I believe they used to give these out to the winners of the school spelling bee."

Maya gave me a sideways glance. I knew what she was thinking. The Doodler—boss of the sixth-graders—blamed everything bad that had happened to him on losing the school spelling bee. Could this be his work?

"This is interesting," Mrs. Hall said, turning the star over and studying the image on the back.

"Do you know what it is?" I asked.

"No." She tapped her chin. "But it looks familiar. I could swear that a girl visiting from another school asked me about something like this a few years ago. A smart little thing with the same fire in her eyes that you have in yours. But I don't think the symbol she showed me was on a medal."

Near the door, a chair squeaked as it slid across the floor. We all turned to find an empty room—the only trace of whoever had been watching us was an abandoned book in the middle of a table. Whoever had been sitting there had disappeared into the flow of students in the hall.

"Spy," Maya mouthed.

I nodded and turned back to Mrs. Hall. "Do you have any idea what the symbols beneath the protractor mean?"

"They look like letters from an ancient alphabet," the librarian said. She arched one eyebrow—something I'd been trying to do for years with no success. "Have you checked the reference section?"

I caught her meaning right away. The reference section of the library was where they kept books that dealt with facts and figures people needed for research. But it was also the home of one of the most mysterious and knowledgeable people in Ordinary Elementary—the Oracle. If anyone would know what the image meant, it was her.

"What do I owe you for your help?" I asked as Mrs. Hall handed the award back to me.

"Two five-page reports on historical figures who helped introduce the Industrial Revolution," she said. "Complete with bibliographies of all referenced sources."

I gasped.

She smiled. "Only kidding. Just read something fun and suggest it to a friend."

"Sure thing." I tipped my hat, trying to hide my relief. "And you keep slinging stories."

"Wouldn't dream of doing anything else." She reached for her mouse and paused. "Keep a close eye out, Gray. The stomach virus might not be the only dangerous thing going around."

I narrowed my eyes, as anxious as a turkey the day before Thanksgiving. "Have you heard something?"

"Nothing specific," she whispered. "It's just a feeling, but my librarian radar is almost never wrong. Be careful."

"Come on," I said to the twins, tucking the medal into my pocket as I headed toward the back of the library.

The twins paused.

"You two aren't afraid of the Oracle, are you?" I asked.

Jack whispered to his sister.

"She *is* powerful," Maya agreed. "I heard she once made a kid's head explode just by telling him the true meaning of the lyrics to 'The Wheels on the Bus.'"

I scratched my ear. "I thought that song was just about a bus."

Jack whispered and Maya shook her head. "Maybe. But we're not going to ask."

"Fine, stay here and keep watch." I looked straight at Jack. "I don't want anyone sneaking up behind me."

The Oracle was a mysterious figure who answered questions and foretold futures in a shadowy nook at the back of the reference library. Kids sought her advice when there was no one else to turn to.

But like most solutions, hers came with a price. She could demand anything from a piece of tape from the dispenser on a cranky history teacher's desk to a pair of chocolate Cadbury eggs with the creamy centers, or even a simple thank you. She never explained how she set her price, and you never knew what it would be until you got there.

In order to reach her lair, you had to avoid dangerous traps and solve clever puzzles. The last time I visited her, I was nearly buried by an avalanche of globes and had to create a bridge of wooden blocks with states on them by putting them in order of their population.

But this time, even though I kept a careful watch, I didn't spot a single trap. I didn't understand why until I reached the Oracle's desk and found a sheet of flowered stationery taped to the front.

Out Sick.

I couldn't believe my bad luck. Who was I supposed to ask now?

Leaning closer, I spotted a second message written in small print at the bottom of the note.

Until I return, try asking Google,
a Magic 8 Ball, or, you know, a book.

"Fine," I muttered, trudging back to the reference shelves. I was still going to get my answer, but this time the price I'd pay was the old-fashioned kind: looking it up myself.

Walking through the stacks, I tried not to get distracted

by *Famous Quotes by Seventeenth-Century Writers* or *How to Survive a Canadian Winter with only a Pocketknife and a Stick of Chewing Gum.* When I finally reached the section on the history of language, I froze.

Carved into the edge of the wooden shelf was a curved protractor. I reached into my pocket and took out the medal to compare the two images. The one on the shelf didn't have the stars, eye, or symbols, but other than that, it was a perfect match.

The cut looked old— had it been made by the girl who'd come to Mrs. Hall a few years ago?

Quickly, I grabbed a book about ancient alphabets. I opened the cover and frowned. The first page was blank. I turned it and the next page was blank as well. I flipped through the book, growing more confused by the second. Every page was as empty as a package of cookies in a classroom full of sixth graders. Every page except for the last, where a handwritten note read:

You didn't think it would be that easy, did you?

I held the book to my nose and sniffed the spine. Binding glue. I tried the next book, and it was the same. There were only a few books about ancient writing in the school library, but all of them were as blank as the first.

Someone had removed the pages from all the books that could help me translate the symbols on the back of the star and had replaced them with blanks.

"But why go to the trouble of changing the pages when

they could have just taken the books?" I wondered. "And why leave a note?"

Something buzzed softly behind me. I turned to find a small camera attached to the wall a few inches below the ceiling.

"This setup couldn't be any more obvious if they put a nametag on it and sent it to parent-teacher conference," I muttered. "The question is, was it meant specifically for me, or did I just stumble onto something much bigger?"

I shoved the books back onto the shelf and hurried to the front of the library as fast as I could without running, which would earn a stern warning from Mrs. Hall the first time and a quick trip out the door if it happened again.

The twins huddled with me behind a rack of paperbacks.

"What happened?" Maya asked. "Did you learn anything?"

"Maybe," I said, looking carefully around. "But definitely not anything I expected. Let's go to the computer lab and do some online sleuthing."

Jack frowned, and his stomach growled so loud it sounded like he'd swallowed an electric train.

I checked the clock. Only twenty minutes until the end of lunch. I patted him on the shoulder. "Okay. Food now, sleuthing after school."

CHAPTER 4
Now You Have It, Now You Don't

On the mean streets of Ordinary Elementary, a kid has to know who they can trust. On a reliability scale of one to ten, Maya, Jack, and the librarian were fifteens, while "Let's Make a Deal" Larry was a three: somewhere between the janitor's cat, Slayer, and a kindergartner named Declan Thurman who swore he had a pet unicorn named Bubbles who took swim lessons from the Tooth Fairy.

For the rest of the afternoon, thoughts of the award in my pocket gnawed at my brain like a hungry toddler with a chicken nugget Happy Meal. Our old teacher, Ms. Morgan, had been replaced by a substitute named Ms. Devencourt. She was nice but mostly gave us assignments and then read books on her phone, which left me plenty of time to stew in my own thoughts.

Like different puzzles mixed up in the same box, there

were too many pieces that didn't fit together. Why would someone hide a spelling bee medal in a wall? If I had won the medal, I would have worn it for a month and then hung it on the refrigerator where my parents would see it every time they made a sandwich. And why had they scratched the strange symbol onto the back?

Then there was the mysterious girl who'd asked Mrs. Hall about the same symbol, the carving of it on the library shelf, and the empty reference books.

I didn't know what any of it meant yet, but I was determined to find out.

Curling my arm over it so no one else could see, I placed the medal on my desk and ran my fingers over the symbol on the back as I considered the possibilities.

By the time the final bell rang, I still had more questions than answers. But I also had a plan, starting with—

"Graysen Foxx," said a smooth voice as I stepped out of the classroom.

It was Larry "Let's Make a Deal" Torrance—the best dressed kid and slipperiest trader in all of Ordinary Elementary. Known for swindling students out of their best Pokémon cards and snacks, Larry was a fixture on the corner of Kindergarten Lane and First Grade Avenue. So what was he doing all the way up in the fifth-grade suburbs?

"A little out of your neighborhood, aren't you?" I asked.

Larry smiled and brushed an invisible cookie crumb off the sleeve of his perfectly pressed lime-green dress shirt.

"I hear you made a killing with the treasure of Principal Redbeard."

"I'm not trading any of it to you," I said, patting the elastic sticky hand I always kept clipped to my belt. "I'm returning those toys to their original owners. Any that I can't return are going to people they can really help. Which doesn't include you."

Larry grinned. "I can wait. Everybody needs something sometime. When they do, Lucky Larry is open twenty-four seven."

I started to walk by him, eager to research the symbols, but he stopped me with an arm around my shoulder. "I'm not here about Pokémon cards. I've got something for you."

"I'm not interested in any of your stale gummy worms," I said, brushing his arm away.

"Maybe not," he blurted. "But what about this?"

At first, I thought the open folder he pressed into my hands contained maps for a video game. Pages of graph paper were covered with intricately labeled rooms, hallways, and levels. It wasn't until I looked closer that I realized they were hand-drawn blueprints of our school.

Unlike more modern schools, Ordinary Elementary was a sprawling two-story brick building with staircases, basements, and sections that had been added and changed over the years. There were also hidden passages and tunnels that I had only recently discovered. The plans showed not only the secret passages I knew about, but at least a dozen others I'd never heard of.

"These are amazing," I said, flipping through the pages.

As quickly as he'd given me the folder, Larry snatched it away. His eyes gleamed. "Interested?"

"Yeah!" I gasped, not even trying to hide my excitement. "Where did you get those?"

"Not important," he said. "What matters is that I have them, you want them, and I can make them yours for one low price."

"How much?" I asked, mentally cataloging everything I could offer. I'd never collected Pokémon cards, and Jack ate most of my snacks. But I had a pretty good comic book collection—some signed by the artists—a bunch of video games, and—

"Wait," I said, sensing a trap. "If this is about Principal Redbeard's treasure, I told you I won't—"

Larry waved his hand. "I'm not interested in any of that. I mean, I am, but not today."

"Then what?" I asked, honestly confused. "Those maps could be invaluable in my treasure hunting. Name your price."

"It's not much," he said. "Honestly, I feel like a sucker for not asking ten times more." He glanced down at my pants pocket, where I could feel the weight of the spelling bee medal. "I'm looking for a star-shaped medal with a picture of a bee on the front."

My tongue stuck to the top of my mouth like gum to the bottom of an old sneaker. When I managed to peel it off, my voice was hoarse and gravelly. "How do you know about that?"

Larry shrugged. "What can I say? It's a collectible. Word gets around. But I want it and you want the maps. So, do we have a deal?"

I folded my arms. Something smelled fishy, and it wasn't just the tuna casserole the cafeteria had served for lunch. "As long as I've known you, the only thing you've been interested in trading for is cards, candy, and comics. When did you get interested in antiques?"

He rolled his eyes. I'd never seen him so smug. "Let's just say I'm expanding my interests."

I didn't believe him for a second. Someone had put him up to this. "Who are you working for? Is it the same person who gave you the maps?"

"Don't worry about that." Larry rubbed one of his polished black dress shoes on the back of his pants. "Do you want the maps or not?"

"I do. But first I want to know who hired you." I tugged down my fedora and edged to the side of the hall. "How much are they paying you?"

He looked up and down the hallway. "I'll level with you. I don't care about the spelling bee thingy. But *some* people do. And they are the kind of people who don't take no for an answer."

"The Doodler?" I asked. "Raven?"

Larry gave a strangled laugh, and I realized the kid wasn't smug. He was scared. "The people who hired me

27

make the Doodler look like a toddler in a sandbox. They have juice, and not the kind you drink for breakfast. The kind that can get you a permanent spot at the front of the lunch line—for life. Or that makes sure you don't get out of this joint until you're old enough to drive."

I pulled the award out of my pocket and shook it in his face. "Tell your friends this is a part of our school's history," I snarled. "It isn't for sale. If they have a problem with that, they can talk to me in person."

"You're making a mistake," Larry said. He looked around nervously again, then lunged forward to grab the medal. But I held it out of his reach.

"Out of my way!" shouted a voice from behind me.

I turned to see a kid sprinting through a group of students straight toward me. At first I thought the kid was wearing a clown mask, but as they got closer I could see that it was actual clown makeup and a red rubber nose.

Before I could react to the unusual sight, the clown— who didn't look any older than six or seven—did a forward flip, yanked the medal out of my hand in midair, and landed on their feet before ducking into a group of laughing fourth graders.

"Get back here!" I yelled, racing after the thief.

"You should have taken the deal," Larry called.

I'd talk to him more later, but first I had to catch up with the pint-sized performer before they delivered my antiquity to their employer or sold it on the black market outside the

cafeteria where lost gloves moved
as fast as PB&J sandwiches.

The clown was sur-
prisingly quick and
nimble for having such puny
legs—they had the advantage
of being low to the ground,
which let them duck under
bigger students and dodge
through narrow openings like
a determined shopper on
Black Friday morning.

I unclipped my sticky
hand and flicked my wrist to retrieve
the stolen loot, but the clown zigged at the last second and
disappeared around a corner. Swinging around after them, I
nearly ran into Maya and Jack, my sneakers skidding on the
recently waxed tile floor.

"What's going on?" Maya asked.

I pointed, trying to catch my breath. "Clown. Stole.
Medal."

Jack didn't hesitate, his feet a blur as he chased after the
high-tailing hoodlum.

Looking back, the clown saw the Ghost catching up and
gave a *yeep* of terror.

"Don't worry," Maya said. "They'll never get away."

But when we finally caught up with Jack, he was

standing with a befuddled expression halfway down an empty hall.

"You didn't let the clown escape, did you?" I asked.

Maya shook her head. "Nobody's faster than my twin."

Jack whispered to his sister and pointed to an opening near the floor.

I knelt to examine an air vent that someone had removed the cover from. It barely looked big enough for a cat to squeeze into. "The clown went down there?"

Jack whispered to his sister and held up a single Spider-Man sneaker.

"He grabbed the clown's leg as they were disappearing into the vent," Maya said. "But the kid wiggled out of their shoe and got away."

"Any chance you could go in after them?" I asked, eying the tiny opening.

Jack shook his head with a shudder.

"He's been feeling claustrophobic since he got trapped in the wolf costume," Maya explained.

Clearly whoever wanted the medal hadn't been willing to take no for an answer. I studied the shoe, feeling like a world-class dope for not having seen something like this coming. "It's a children's thirteen and a half," I muttered. "Exactly the right size shoe for a first grader—or possibly a small, but speedy second-grade spy."

As if by magic, a girl with long dark hair appeared, leaning against a scarecrow decoration. "Did I hear somebody mention my network?"

Lizzy Stonebrook, queen of the second-grade spies, glided toward us as silently as a ghost in Heelys and studied the open vent. "What happened?"

I looked at the twins. Could we trust her? Lizzy said that her spies weren't working for Raven anymore. But alliances could change as quickly as Jake could change costumes between scenes in a play. "Something important was just stolen from me," I said. "And I think the kid who swiped it might have been one of yours."

Lizzy frowned. "What did this supposed spy look like?"

"I'm not sure," I admitted. "They were disguised as a clown, but they were wearing this." I held out the sneaker.

Lizzy quickly examined the shoe, then handed it back. "It wasn't one of mine."

"How can you be sure?" Maya asked.

Lizzy tapped the bottom of the sneaker and the Spider-Man head on the side flashed briefly. "No member of my network would ever wear light-up shoes—and clowns freak me out."

"So, a second grader who isn't one of the spies?" I suggested. "Or maybe a first grader with large feet?"

Jack and Maya whispered back and forth.

Maya frowned. "Jack says that none of them would be fast enough to get away from him."

I folded my arms, remembering the librarian's warning to keep an eye out. "We're missing something, and it's not just the medal."

CHAPTER 5
A Familiar Face

In elementary school, there's a new story every
morning, a new kickball game every afternoon,
and a new opportunity around every corner.
The key is knowing which corners to check.

Before school the next day, Maya, Jack, and I held a
secret meeting at the back of the playground with Cameron,
the captain of the first-grade guard, and his friends Blake
and Asher. These days, Asher was going by the nickname
"Skittles" because of the candy trick he'd used a few weeks
earlier to help me escape the Doodler's guards.

Blake cradled the clown's footwear in her hand like
Prince Charming holding Cinderella's glass slipper. "I'm sure
I'd remember if I'd seen anyone wearing one of these."

Skittles took the sneaker from Blake and bounced it
against his palm, making Spider-Man's head flash on and
off. "Do you have the other one? They'd go great with my
superhero shorts."

"Sorry," I said. "This is it."

"That's okay." He laughed, his curls bouncing like tiny

brown springs. "Maybe I could wear this on one foot and a bunny slipper on the other one for Silly Shoes Day."

"Keep it," I said. "I'm pretty sure it's not going to help us find the person we're searching for."

Cameron, the only first grader I knew who wore a suit to school every day, straightened his tie. "Is this about what happened after school yesterday?"

"You know about that?" I asked, rubbing my mouth.

"Of course," Cameron said. "The whole school's talking about how an acrobatic clown stole a rare artifact from you and disappeared from sight in front of everyone."

"Was it really made of solid gold?" Blake asked, her eyes shining.

Skittles nodded. "Is it worth millions of dollars?"

"Not exactly," I said, feeling as vulnerable as the last Reese's Peanut Butter Cup in a Halloween bowl. I preferred to do my adventuring out of sight, but that didn't look like it was going to be possible this time. "If you hear anything about the kid who took it, can you let me know?"

"Sure thing," Cameron said. He tugged at the cuffs of his shirtsleeves, then stood as tall as he could. "The first-grade guard is at your service."

As the three kids left, Jack whispered to his sister.

"He does look sharp," Maya agreed. "But I'd hate to be the one paying his dry cleaning bill."

"Whoever's masterminding this knew I'd go to the library and that I'd refuse to trade with Larry," I said. "But what are they up to?"

Maya snorted. "If that clown wasn't so small, I'd swear it was Rotten Raven in disguise."

"Did someone mention my name?" asked a voice as sweet as an afternoon bake sale. Sure, it was sugary sweet, but I knew everything it was selling came with a price tag.

I turned to see my archnemesis herself lurking behind us like a gym teacher about to make their students take a surprise fitness test.

Raven turned to Maya and waggled one finger. "You got my name wrong, though. It's *Red* Raven. Not *Rotten* Raven."

"You can call yourself whatever you want," Maya said. "But stealing the spelling bee medal was pure rotten. So that's what I'm calling you until you give it back."

"A medal, hmm?" Raven said. "I didn't know what you lost until now. Thanks for the info."

"Nice bluff," I said. "But we both know you're involved. Stealing things is your calling card."

Raven tsked. "I've taken many things from you, but the first time I heard about the medal was this morning. Everyone's talking about how the great 'Gray Fox' was beaten by a kid in a clown costume. Très embarrassing, Graysen."

Raven had done lot of things, but I'd never known her to tell an outright lie. "If you didn't take it, who did?"

"How would I know?" She laughed. "Maybe you should find the kid who won it and ask them."

"Right," Maya snarled. "And I'm sure you didn't steal the painting we found, either."

"That *was* me." Raven rolled her eyes. "But can it really

be called stealing if someone hands it to me of their own free choice?"

"You said you'd changed after we worked together to find Principal Redbeard's treasure," I said. "I thought you'd stopped only thinking about yourself."

"I did change. For a while. But it's too much fun to see the look on your face when you realize I've outsmarted you again." Raven's eyes gleamed. "We need each other, Foxx. Without me keeping you on your toes, you'd spend all day dusting artifacts and making notes in your dumb journal. And without you to take advantage of, I'd be bored."

"She's lying," Maya said, balling her fists. "She must be behind this."

Raven laughed again, holding her hand up in a solemn three-fingered salute. "I swear I didn't take your dumb spelling bee medal. But if I hear anything about who did, I'll let you know." She turned and walked toward the school, calling over her shoulder, "Of course, you're all invited to join my class for pizza after we win the Halloween decorating contest."

Jack's eyes got big. He started to whisper to Maya, but she shook her head. "Don't even think about it."

"What now?" Maya asked once it was just the three of us again. "If Raven's telling the truth and Lizzy's spics weren't involved, that only leaves the Doodler."

"Maybe. I could totally see him deciding this would make up for the spelling bee he lost in third grade. But it doesn't feel like his work. If he wanted the medal, he'd just send a couple of his sixth-grade goons to take it." I wiped my palms on my shirt. "We need to try another angle. Instead of hoping that the thief will lead us to the medal, maybe learning more about the medal will lead us to the thief."

"Good thinking," Maya said. "We can start by searching the internet for the symbols scratched into the back of the star."

I scuffed the toe of my sneaker across the playground gravel. "That *would* be a good plan," I said. "Only there's a small problem."

Jack whispered to his sister.

"Of course he knows what they looked like," Maya said. "Graysen documents everything in his field journal."

"Usually that's true," I said, shuffling my feet. "But school was about to start when we found the medal. Then I got distracted by the books in the library. Then I was going to Google the letters beneath the symbol when Larry showed up, and . . ."

Maya's eyes narrowed. "You didn't copy the image on the back of the star into your field journal?"

I shook my head. It was the kind of rookie mistake an experienced adventurer should never let happen, and I'd been kicking myself all night over it.

"What clues do we have left?" Maya asked.

Jack made a zero with his thumb and first finger.

It seemed that way. But something Raven had said got me thinking.

"What if we track down the kid who won the award?"

Maya frowned. "It's been almost a hundred years since the contest. That person's probably been dead for years."

Jack whispered urgently in her ear.

Maya sighed. "No, he doesn't want us to talk to dead people." She looked up at me. "Do you?"

"Of course not," I said. "I'm not suggesting that we track down the actual person. But if we can figure out who won the award in the first place, it could give us an idea of why they hid it. And maybe even a clue about who took it."

The twins looked at each other and nodded.

"Okay," Maya said. "Where do we start?"

I grinned. "When the lunch bell rings, meet me at the trophy case."

•   •   •

The trophy case was a giant wooden box attached to the wall just outside the gymnasium doors. Crowding the shelves were trophies, awards, and ribbons for everything from basketball to baking contests, along with team pictures so old some of them had almost completely faded.

"Over here," Maya said, pointing to a row of dusty wooden plaques on the bottom shelf that were squeezed between bowling trophies and drama awards.

"Spelling bee winners," she read. "That's what we're looking for, isn't it?"

"Yes." I studied the names tracking the winners back to the earliest years of the school. But the metal plate for 1927 was so tarnished I couldn't read the name even with my nose

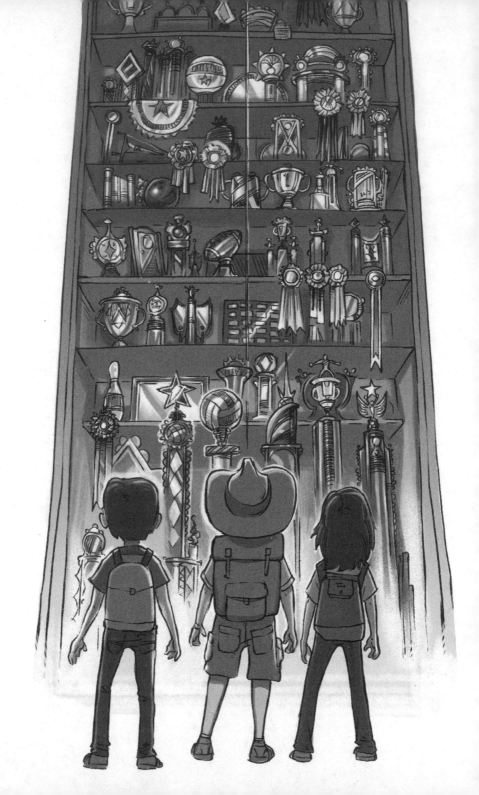

pressed against the glass. "We have to find out who has the key to open this."

Before the words had completely left my mouth, Jack pulled a staple remover and a mechanical pencil out of his backpack. He poked one side of the staple remover into the keyhole and prodded the lock with the tip of the pencil until it twisted open.

"How did you learn to do that?" I asked as Jack slid back one of the glass panels.

"YouTube videos," Maya said. "He broke into our pantry when he was five and ate half a dozen freshly baked conchas."

Jack shrugged.

Careful not to disturb any of the other awards, I reached into the trophy case and took out the first spelling bee plaque. Even up close, the name was impossible to make out. I tried polishing it with the sleeve of my jacket, but it didn't help.

Jack whispered to Maya.

"It *does* look like a dead end," Maya said.

"Maybe not." I rooted around in my archaeology supplies until I found a small glass bottle and an old gym sock. I poured some of the liquid onto the sock and rubbed it across the plate.

"Is that acid?" Maya asked.

"Vinegar," I said. "But it is acidic, which makes it great for cleaning metal."

Slowly, the corrosion on the plate dissolved.

"H-U-B-E-R-T," I read as the letters appeared. "Hubert."

The rest of the tarnish cleared, revealing a last name we were all familiar with: *Sullivan.*

"That was Principal Redbeard's last name," Maya whispered. "Do you think the two of them were related?"

There was one way to find out. We returned the plaque to the case and locked it, then hurried down the hall to the computer lab.

An internet search of the name "Hubert Sullivan" returned thousands of results. But when I added "Ordinary Elementary" and "spelling bee," only a single link remained.

"That's it," Maya said as I clicked on the link, opening a scanned image of an old newspaper article.

Above the article was a black-and-white picture of a boy standing between his parents and an old man. Maya reached over my shoulder to zoom in. Dressed in a jacket and tie that made even Cameron's suit look shabby, the boy was holding the exact medal I had found, hanging from the end of a shiny blue ribbon.

But it wasn't the medal or the boy that drew my attention. With fingers trembling like a video game player about to beat the final level, I zoomed in on the stern-looking old man standing beside the boy.

"Is it just me," I murmured, "or does that look like—"

"The creepy old man from the painting," Maya said. "The one who gave all the money to the school."

CHAPTER 6
Unexpected Company

School friendships are like Minecraft blocks. Some are stuck together so tight you couldn't break them apart with a diamond pick. Some fit together one way, break apart, and get put back in a different direction. And then, occasionally, you connect a couple of blocks that seem like they should never fit together, look at what you've built, and think, "This might just work."

The article itself was short and didn't tell us much more than we already knew. Hubert Sullivan, a sixth grader, won the first annual Ordinary Elementary School Spelling Bee by correctly spelling the word "inexplicable"—which felt surprisingly appropriate to our current situation.

The caption beneath the picture was much more interesting.

Hubert Sullivan with his parents, Ronald and Phillis Sullivan, and grandfather, wealthy businessman, Howard Sullivan III.

So that was the old man's name. Another search revealed that Hubert's great-grandfather Howard Sullivan II had been one of the wealthiest businessmen in the world in the early 1900s, running everything from paper mills to railroads.

His son, Howard Sullivan III—who had donated the money to help build our school—expanded his father's wealth even more until the family was worth nearly a billion dollars, which was unheard of at the time.

"Wow!" Maya said. "No wonder Hubert left his medal under the stage. His parents probably replaced it with one made of gold and diamonds."

Jack opened his mouth, but Maya didn't need to hear what he was going to say. "No, I don't think that's under the stage too."

Jack opened a new tab on the browser and entered all the names we'd been talking about into a genealogy site. A second later, a family tree appeared.

I nodded. "Smart."

Two rows under Hubert was the name *Sylvester Sullivan*.

"That's *Principal* Sullivan," I said. "Principal Redbeard is Hubert's grandson!"

Maya frowned. "If he was so rich, why was he working as the principal of an elementary school?"

"Maybe he just loved the school," I said. "I mean, his family helped build it."

At the bottom of the genealogy page were a bunch of pictures. Maya clicked on one of them. "Look. It's the same painting we found under the stage."

I bent closer. "Zoom in," I said, feeling my archaeology senses start to tingle again.

As Maya enlarged the picture, I saw something I hadn't noticed in the original. "Look at the ring he's wearing."

Maya zoomed in as far as she could without losing focus, and there on the old man's finger was the exact image that had been scratched into the back of the medal. It was a little fuzzy, but I was almost positive that I'd be able to translate the symbols beneath it.

"How do we print that out?" I asked.

A weaselly boy in a video game T-shirt and cargo pants stood up from behind a nearby computer monitor. "I can help."

"Klart," I said, my stomach as tight as the lid of the Tupperware container my mom used to store leftover sloppy joes. "You've been spying on us."

Klart Kirby was the Doodler's tech guru and second-in-command of the Venerable but Quick-Tempered Order of the Sixth Graders.

"Suddenly everything makes sense," I continued. "The Doodler's been behind this all along. Did he think stealing someone else's medal would make people forget he never won a spelling bee himself?"

I reached for my elastic sticky hand, but the Doodler's assistant held out his palms. "There's no need for violence. I'm not here on business."

"Sure," I barked. "And your boss doesn't smell like day-old Sharpies."

Klart laughed. "He totally does. But he's been out of school sick since last Thursday." He looked toward the door and dropped his voice. "I'm sort of running things until he gets back."

"If you weren't spying on us, why were you hiding back there?" Maya asked.

Klart turned around his monitor, revealing a game of Rocket League still playing on the screen. "The computers here are set to block any video games. I didn't want anyone to know I got around the filters."

Jack whispered to Maya, and Klart raised an eyebrow.

Maya clicked her tongue against the roof of her mouth, giving her brother a dark look. "He wants to know if you can show him how to get onto Roblox from here."

"Sure." Klart grinned, walking around the table.

"Hold it right there," I said, quickly closing our search screens so he couldn't see what we'd been up to. "Maybe you're telling the truth and maybe you aren't. But after the way you and the rest of the Doodler's goons treated me, there's no way I'll ever trust you."

Klart nodded. "I get that. It was a mean thing to do, and I never would have if the Doodler hadn't made me." He scratched the back of his head. "I mean we're all stuck here together for seven years. Why spend that time picking on each other, right?"

Maya crossed her arms. "Are you saying our grades should form an alliance?"

"No way!" Klart said, shaking with laughter. "I mean us sixth graders have been here, like forever. We totally run the school, and nothing is going to change that. But just because we're the bosses doesn't mean we have to pick on you shrimps all the time."

He pointed to our computer screen. "We can even help each other out now and then. Like, I can show you how to print the picture of that ring you're all excited about."

I sneered. "So you *were* listening."

"I mean, it was sort of hard to miss," Klart said. "It's not like you three were being quiet, which technically is one of the biggest rules of the computer lab. Right up there with not hacking the network. And the three of you sort of have a reputation for finding cool stuff. So . . ."

"It doesn't matter," Maya said. "You don't know what the ring is or why it's important. And we shut the browsers."

"About that." Klart bit his bottom lip. "You shut the browser on this computer. But you didn't actually close it."

"What are you talking about?" I asked, staring at the screen. "I'm no tech geek, but how can closing a browser not close a browser?"

"When someone else is watching what you do on your computer." He tapped a small blinking icon on the bottom of the screen. "It looks like Goldilocks has been snooping around the Three Bears' house. And my guess is she's probably finished eating all your porridge."

From the corner of the room, a chair squeaked.

As we raced around the computers, another person popped up from behind her computer screen.

"Hello, Gray," Raven said, brushing the red hair out of her eyes. "What a coincidence running into you again."

CHAPTER 7

Messages from the Past

*Treasure hunting is like the family TV.
You never know who's watching until
you try to change the channel.*

"Your being here is no coincidence," I said. "You've been spying on us again."

"You followed us," Maya said.

Raven shrugged. "Technically, I got here before any of you. Including the Doodler's hitman."

Klart huffed. "I've never hit anybody."

"Maybe you got here before us," Maya said, pointing to the picture of Howard Sullivan's ring on Raven's screen. "But you *were* spying."

Raven shrugged again. "You've got me there."

"Wait," I said. Like a broken calculator, things weren't adding up. "We didn't even know we were going to come to the lab until we found Hubert's name in the trophy case. How could you have gotten here before us? And how did you know which computer to track?"

Raven licked her lips. "Isn't it obvious? I mean, if you were looking for information about an old award, the first place you'd check is the trophy case. After that, I assumed you'd need to search the internet. It was just a matter of time before you showed up here. And it made sense that the computer you'd use was the first one inside the door."

It was a diabolically brilliant plan. Maybe I'd under-estimated the power of her true evil genius.

Klart narrowed his eyes. "Nice try. But according to the icons in your toolbar, you hacked the network filtering soft-ware the same way I did. Only instead of using it to play games, you're using it to watch what everyone else is doing on their computers."

Jack and Maya both gasped.

"Is that true?" I asked. What he was suggesting seemed too low even for my archnemesis.

Raven slumped in her chair. "After the second-grade spies stopped working with me, I didn't have any other place to go for information."

Klart shook his head. "When Principal Luna hears about this, you're toast. This kind of thing stays on your permanent record forever."

Raven sneered. "You hacked the network too."

"To play games," Klart said. "Not to spy."

Raven dropped her head. "Please don't tell anyone," she begged, actually looking sorry for once. "I knew it was wrong, but I couldn't figure out any other way to get information. I swear I'll delete the software and never spy on anyone's computer ever again."

Klart looked at me, Maya, and Jack. "It's your call, man. I mean this is some pretty juicy information, and from what I've heard, she'd probably use it against you."

"If we tell, you'll get in trouble too," Maya said.

"It wouldn't be the first time."

For a minute, I was tempted to turn them both in. Klart had helped the Doodler chase me around the school, and Raven had never been afraid to get me in trouble if it helped her get a treasure first. But I shook my head. "If you promise to stop using the school's computers to play games and Raven agrees to delete her spy software, plus everything she found, and never use any of it to hurt anyone, we'll forget this happened."

Klart grinned. "Cool!"

Raven narrowed her eyes. "Why are you being so nice? Is this a trap?"

"No trap," I said. "We've all done things we shouldn't have."

I checked with Maya and Jack. "Do you two agree?"

Jack whispered to his sister, and Maya gave a mischievous grin.

"We won't tell anyone either. As long as you take the painting out of your classroom and return it to ours, where it belongs."

"Deal," Raven said at once. "And since you three are

helping me, I'll even tell you what the symbols at the bottom of that ring are."

I squeaked like a chew toy in the mouth of a hungry schnauzer. "You know?"

"Of course," Raven said, regaining her usual smug smile. "What do you think I was doing while you and Fortnite boy were trying to negotiate school peace?"

"It was Rocket League," Klart said. "Fortnite is for posers. And if you tell anyone I was being nice to a fifth grader, I will hack into the office system and change all your grades to Fs. Plus, I'll add a note to every one of your report cards that says you make random chicken noises during the middle of class."

Raven made a *pfft* sound. "I'll change your record to move you back to fourth grade."

"You can't do that," Klart said, but I could tell he wasn't sure.

"Both of you stop threatening each other and show us what you found," I said, as excited as a teacher with a new pack of dry erase markers.

"Okay, let me show you what I found before we all miss lunch," Raven said. "Although, I hear the lunch lady is trying a new recipe that includes fried bologna cutlets and boiled eggplant, so it might not be such a big loss."

"Forget lunch and show us," I said.

Jack's stomach growled.

"Okay, don't forget lunch," I corrected. "But tell us anyway."

Raven switched
tabs on her browser.
"I realized right away
that the symbols had
to be letters from an
ancient alphabet."

"I knew it," I said.
"Greek?"

Raven shook her head.
"Older."

"Coptic?" Klart suggested.

We all turned to stare at him.

"What?" he asked. "Just because I like video games
doesn't mean I'm not smart."

Jack nodded emphatically.

"Enough suspense already," I said, feeling like a kid who
has to wait for their boring uncle to finish talking about the
responsibilities of getting older before opening their birth-
day presents. "Did you figure out what they are or not?"

Raven sniffed. "I wouldn't be showing you this if I
hadn't." She opened an image search, pasted in a picture
of the symbols on the ring, and immediately got a hit.
"Phoenician!"

Maya and Jack looked at each other with confused expressions.

"The Phoenicians were an ancient civilization," I explained. "They lived in the Mediterranean area from about
1500 to 300 BC."

Jack whispered to Maya and she nodded. "Yep, even older than Dad."

"They were amazing ship builders who sailed to places like Greece, Egypt, and Mesopotamia, trading goods and sharing the cultures of each of the places they visited. But even more important, they created the world's oldest verified alphabet."

"You just know that off the top of your head?" Klart asked.

Raven rolled her eyes. "He's a total history geek."

Maya looked at the picture of the ring. "Are you saying that's some kind of ancient relic?"

"Definitely not," Raven said. "And keep your voice down unless you want the whole school to know what we found. We still don't know who stole your medal, remember?"

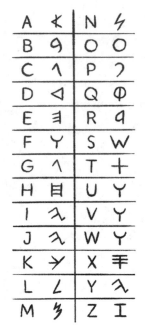

She had a point. Whoever vandalized the library books and hired the crafty clown might not be happy about what we'd discovered.

"Okay," Maya said quietly. "Go on."

Raven cracked her knuckles and began to type. "The symbols are from a version of the Phoenician alphabet modified by the Greeks to include vowels."

She typed a series of letters on the screen. "When I matched the symbols to our alphabet, I got this."

Ainmo repus aitnegilletni

"That sounds like Latin," I said.

Jack whispered to Maya.

"He thinks it's a spell for keeping away aliens."

"That's what I thought," Raven said. "The Latin part. Not the alien repulsion spell." She opened a Latin-to-English translator. But when she pasted the letters into it, a message appeared that said *Not Recognized.*

"If it's not Latin, what is it?" Klart asked.

Raven brushed her hair out of her eyes. "No clue."

Was she bluffing to keep us from learning the truth?

I tried it myself with the same results.

"You thought I was trying to trick you?" Raven asked, sounding offended.

We all stared at her, and she tossed up her hands. "Okay, that does sound like something I'd do."

Jack whispered to Maya again and Klart leaned toward me. "Why doesn't the kid talk out loud?"

"He does," I said. "But only in the dark—or inside of a wolf costume where no one can see his face."

Maya frowned. "Jack wants to know why you went through all of this only to tell us you have no idea what's on the ring?"

"I said I knew what the symbols were," Raven snapped. "I didn't say I'd figured out what they meant. But that's still pretty impressive considering I only had a few minutes to work before you discovered I was spying on you."

Klart looked at me. "Any ideas, super sleuth?"

A code? A puzzle? An anagram? I tried to consider the symbols from the perspective of whoever designed it.

"The letters have to mean something, or they wouldn't have bothered putting them on the image. But they wore it on a ring, which means they weren't afraid of showing it publicly, so it wasn't too top secret."

Klart leaned toward Jack. "Is he going somewhere with this, or does he just like to sound smart?"

Jack rocked his hand back and forth.

"Shush," Maya hissed.

I tapped my fingers on the desk, mentally rearranging the letters on the screen. "A complex cypher doesn't make sense. It has to be something secret enough that the average person wouldn't figure it out, but simple enough that a solution would be—Wait!" I slapped my forehead. "The symbols are Phoenician, right?"

Raven nodded.

"Then we're missing one important piece." I pulled out a sheet of paper and quickly redrew the letters. "Try typing this into the Latin translator: *intelligentia super omnia*."

"That's just the message backward," Maya said.

I laughed. "Not to the Phoenicians. They wrote their words and sentences from right to left. For us it's backward. But for them it was forward."

Raven typed in the letters and hit enter. Immediately a translation appeared. She read the three words out loud. "Intelligence above all."

Instantly, the computers made a strange hissing sound

and every screen in the room turned off. The lights overhead flickered.

"What's happening?" Klart said. "What did you do?"

I unclipped my sticky hand, sensing a trap. "Is this part of your spyware?"

"I didn't do anything, and this definitely isn't coming from anything I installed on the network," Raven said. She reached for the mouse, but before she could touch it, every monitor turned on, filling the room with a blinding white glare.

"*Congratulations, seekers of knowledge,*" a deep voice boomed. At the same time, the words scrolled across all of the monitors.

> *By speaking the secret phrase of power,*
> *you have proven yourselves worthy to pursue*
> *a treasure greater than any you can imagine.*
> *Complete the quest first and the grail is yours.*

I leaned toward Klart. "This isn't one of your video games, is it?"

He shook his head.

"*But beware,*" the voice boomed, "*the path is both difficult and dangerous. Fail any step and you will have proved yourself unworthy to continue.*"

Something that looked like the number two with a line sticking out from the front flashed on each computer. Then the lights stopped flickering and the screens all returned to normal.

CHAPTERS 8
The Hunt Is On

The true judge of a person's character is what
they do when they discover there are five kids
but only three Peanut M&M's left in the bag.

"What was that?" Maya asked. "It said something about
treasure."

Raven clicked on the toolbar of the screen in front of
her, trying to open the message again. "It's gone."

Remembering my mistake with the image on the back
of the spelling bee medal, I grabbed my journal and wrote
down everything I could remember.

Klart leaned over and typed on the keyboard. "I don't
see any software that could send an instant message running
on this computer, even in the background. Can your spyware see where it came from?"

"Let me check," Raven said, opening a new window
and typing in a series of system commands until she finally
shook her head. "There's no history of it coming in from
outside the network."

"So it was someone inside the school pulling a prank,"
I said.

"No." She tried a couple more commands before leaning back and taking a deep breath. "It didn't come from outside. But I don't see any traffic coming from inside either. It's like all the school phones ringing at the same time—when none of them are even plugged in."

Jack whispered to Maya.

"It showed up when you read the translation," Maya said. "He thinks you should try that again."

Raven cleared her throat. "Intelligence above all."

Nothing happened.

She tried a second time, more loudly. Still nothing.

Klart and Maya both repeated the words, but the screen stayed the same.

"It didn't come from outside the school, so it can't be a streaming video or spam," Klart said.

Raven shook her head. "And it wasn't sent from any of the computers on the network."

Klart rubbed his chin. "Which only leaves a program running locally. Only there aren't any."

They were making as many points as the school pencil sharpener, but they were missing the most important one of all. "The person who sent the message signed it."

"I don't remember seeing a name," Maya said as Jack shook his head.

"Not a name. But definitely a signature." I showed them the symbol at the bottom of the message in my open field journal.

"Looks like a negative two," Klart said.

"Close. But it's actually the Phoenician letter I."

He snorted. "Great. Now all we have to do is question every kid in the school whose first or last name starts with I. Ivan, Isaac, Ivy, Isabella—"

"But how many of them spell their names in Phoenician?" I asked. "I don't think it was an initial. I think it was the pronoun I. Like, *I am the person talking to you.*"

"Or eye," Raven said. She clicked on the browser tab with the picture of Howard Sullivan's ring. "Look. The same symbol is inside the eye."

I hadn't noticed it before, but the pupil of the eye in the center of the protractor was definitely the same symbol from the bottom of the message.

"An I inside of an eye," Klart muttered, looking from the field journal to the ring. "So maybe they want us to know they're watching us?"

We all looked nervously around the room.

"What are the chances that whoever sent that message also sent the clown to steal the spelling bee medal?" Maya asked.

"One hundred percent," I said. "They also have to be

the same people who changed the library books so we'd come here to look the information up on the internet."

Raven nodded. "The whole thing was an elaborate setup to get you to come here now."

"To prove we were smart enough to figure it out," I said.

"That we were persistent enough not to give up?" Maya suggested.

Raven smirked. "That we were tricky enough to find out what each other knew."

"Hang on." Klart rubbed a mustache he didn't actually have. "Are you guys saying that message could be, you know, legit? Like, a real treasure?"

An hour earlier, I would have sworn the only person in the school able to pull off something that was both this devious and clever at the same time was the one sitting at the computer in front of me.

Raven must have read my thoughts, because she spun her chair around to face me, scowling. "I didn't do this."

"I believe you," I said. "But if it wasn't you, who was it?"

"Principal Luna?" Maya asked. "She's the one who set up—"

I held up a hand, cutting her off. Klart didn't know about everything that had happened before, and I wasn't sure he should. "It can't be Principal Luna. She already knows she can trust us. But I can't think of anyone else in the school who would know about the medal, be able to scare "Let's Make a Deal" Larry, and have the technical knowledge to send a message even Raven and Klart can't track."

"Am I missing something?" Klart asked.

"Almost definitely," Raven said. She tapped her chin. "What if the person or people behind this don't go to our school? You said that Lizzy and Cameron both agreed the kid in the clown suit wasn't anyone in their grade."

I narrowed my eyes. "No, I didn't."

"Fine." She tossed her hands again. "I heard it when I was spying on you. What matters is that nobody knows who the clown was, Larry was terrified of whoever he was working for, and we all agree that no one else at our school could pull this off. That only leaves one possibility. We're dealing with someone outside of the school."

I had to admit it was the only thing that made sense. "The question is, do we assume their message is a hoax since everything before this was a trick? Or do we take the message seriously because they obviously seem to know what they're doing?"

"Which one is it?" Klart asked. "Is there a treasure or not?"

It was the classic dilemma all treasure hunters eventually faced. "The heart must believe that deep in the vast unknown of elementary schooldom lies Shangri-la, Atlantis— the place somewhere over the rainbow where X marks the spot, the best books are never checked out by someone else, shoes stay tied, and every day is Taco Tuesday."

"Wow," Klart said, looking at Jack and Maya. "That was almost poetic. I can see why you two hang out with him."

Jack nodded.

"But the brain has to measure the cost of searching," I continued. "There's nothing sadder than a broken fifth grader wandering aimlessly from hallway to hallway— hopes shattered, homework unfinished, lunch money gone, all because the big prize was just around the next corner."

Maya shrugged. "He can be sort of a downer when he hasn't eaten."

"There's only way to find out for sure," Raven said. "Follow the clues and see where they lead."

"What kind of clues are we talking about?" Klart asked, pacing around the room. "Is this like that game Clue, where we figure out that Colonel Mustard committed the murder in the dining room with a bazooka? Or are we talking cloak-and-dagger spy stuff?"

"I'm pretty sure there are no bazookas in Clue," Maya said.

I cleared space on a nearby computer desk and took a

map of the school out of my pack. "The first step in any quest is to make a list of—"

"Hold up," Raven said. "Why are we including Klart? He isn't a treasure hunter."

"I could be," Klart said. "If there was enough money involved."

Raven rolled her chair toward me. "There's no reason to include him. He didn't have anything to do with finding the medal or figuring out what it said."

"Look who's talking," Maya snapped. "The only reason you're involved is because you stole the painting and spied on us."

"Which just goes to show how valuable I am," Raven said. "Would you rather have me working with you or working against you?"

"Ha!" Klart said. "From what I've heard, those can both be true at the same time."

Treasure hunting parties were like class sizes. Smaller was almost always better. Every extra kid was another chance to start a mutiny and another bathroom break you had to plan for. But we'd all been here when the message arrived, which meant none of us had any claim to decide who was included or who wasn't.

"We all know about the treasure," I said. "Which means we're all going to be searching for it. We might as well work together."

"Fine," Raven said. "But anything we find gets split evenly. Fifty percent for me and fifty percent for the rest of you."

"Nice try," Klart said. "The only fair way to divide things is in thirds. Each of our groups gets thirty-three percent, with the last one percent going to me since I'm older."

"No way." Maya marched up to the much-bigger Klart until her face was almost touching his chest. "Graysen, Jack, and I did all the work to get here, so we should get most of the treasure."

Jack whispered to his sister, eyes gleaming.

Maya snorted. "The message didn't say anything about the treasure including Lego sets."

Jack folded his arms, waiting.

"Fine. If the treasure includes Legos, you can have them."

"You can have them," Klart said, "as long as I get the cash."

Raven ran her hands through her hair. "This is never going to work. None of you trust me—which is actually pretty understandable. I have serious doubts about working with third graders. And no one with any sense at all should trust the Doodler's second-in-command."

"I told you, he's not involved in this," Klart said.

Maya listened carefully as Jack leaned toward her.

"The Doodler will definitely get involved when he hears the word treasure," she said.

Klart shrugged.

"What do you suggest?" I asked.

Raven smirked. "The usual. Everyone for themselves, and may the best—or sneakiest—treasure hunter win."

CHAPTER 9
The Treasure Hunter's Guild

"What goes around, comes around" is true for both how you treat other people and tetherball. Just make sure that if something's coming really fast toward your face, you remember to duck.

The minute school ended, Maya, Jack, and I headed to the playground to plan our hunt. We had to get started fast if we wanted to stay ahead of the others. Even without her spyware, Raven had plenty of connections, which meant she probably had at least a dozen leads already. And there was a reason the Doodler trusted Klart to get any and all info.

"Um, Gray," Maya said as we stepped out the back door of the school.

The black asphalt that was usually filled by kids shooting hoops, kicking balls, playing four square, and messing around was now covered with tents, wooden stalls, hay bales, pumpkins, and a bounce house shaped like a haunted mansion.

My first thought was that a band of nearby wandering

traders had set up their village in the middle of the basket-ball courts. My second thought, which actually made a lot more sense, was that the PTA was preparing for the fall carnival that would be running over the weekend.

"We can't meet here," Maya said. "Anyone could overhear us."

"What about there?" I pointed to a spot between a ring toss game and a face painting booth.

Jack shook his head.

"Too crowded," Maya said. "We need to meet you-know-where." I felt my stomach jump like a frog in a pond full of storks.

Jack gave me a pitying look and whispered to his sister.

Maya nodded. "He's definitely still afraid to go into the girls' bathroom."

"I'm not," I sputtered, giving them both a stern glare.

While searching for Principal Redbeard's treasure, the three of us had discovered a secret explorer's guild beneath the school. The round room was decorated with tall wooden pillars, tapestries on the walls, enormous bookshelves, desks, tables, and even a fireplace—the perfect gathering spot for adventurers to plan a treasure hunt.

The only problem was that to get there, you had to follow a slippery, circular staircase hundreds of feet underground, climb over piles of trash, and carefully follow a passageway where you could get lost forever if you took a single wrong turn. Clearly, whoever built it wasn't thinking about convenience.

Worst of all, you also had to move tiles into a secret pattern on the wall of . . . *the girls' bathroom.*

Maya patted my back. "It's okay to say you're scared. Admitting your fears is the first step in overcoming them."

I licked my lips. "Really?"

"Sure. Just say, 'Even though I'm a heroic fifth-grade treasure hunter who faces danger head-on, I'm too terrified to go into a room dozens of kindergarteners use every day.'"

She had no shame. "Fine," I muttered. "Let's go."

Maya checked to make sure no one was inside and moved the wall tiles while I wiped cold sweat from my forehead and reminded myself it was only a bathroom.

The minute the secret entrance swung open, Jack hopped into the hole and started down the spiral staircase.

"Wait," I called, turning on my flashlight.

The first time we'd gone down those stairs, we'd done it in the dark, and Maya and I nearly fell to the bottom of the shaft when the steps unexpectedly ended. Ever since then, I'd brought a light.

"Don't worry," Jack called up from the darkness below. "I can see fine."

"He talked our parents into buying him night vision goggles," Maya explained. "Now he wears them every chance he gets."

I guess that made sense for a kid who only felt comfortable talking in the dark.

"They're amazing," Jack called up from below us. "Last

week, I went into our backyard at night and pretended I was shopping in a grocery store with no electricity."

I looked at Maya, but she only shook her head. "Why would you do that?"

"To prepare for the zombie shopocalypse."

"Don't you mean the zombie *apocalypse*?" I asked.

"Nah. Surviving zombies is easy," Jack said, his feet clanging against the metal stairs. "They're slow, not very smart, and falling apart. What you need to worry about are all the shoppers hoarding toilet paper, snack cakes, and beef jerky. That's where *I* come in. As soon as the zombies knock out the power, I'm filling up my cart with Charmin Ultra Soft, Twinkies, and Slim Jims."

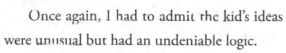

Once again, I had to admit the kid's ideas were unusual but had an undeniable logic.

When we finally walked through the door to the guild room, Raven was already there, reading a book and warming her feet in front of the fireplace.

"Took you long enough," she said.

"What are you doing here?" Maya barked. "This is our room. We're the ones who discovered it."

"Please." Raven closed her book and set it on the table beside her. "This place has been here for years. It doesn't belong to anyone. Besides, I found it seconds after the three of you did."

"Because you followed us," I said. "It's for guild members only."

"A fair point. But technically I found the treasure first, which makes me every bit as much a guild member as you three. Besides"—she turned to Maya—"the only way to get here is through the girls' bathroom, which makes a fairly strong case that even the guild members knew girls are better treasure hunters than boys. Am I right?"

Maya shrugged. "Maybe. But you're not a treasure hunter. You're a treasure stealer."

Raven rolled her eyes. "Po-tay-to, po-tah-to. The point is, I'm here."

"Come on," I said, turning around. "Let's go. This place stinks like pettiness, greed, and cherry lip gloss."

"It's the fireplace," Raven said. "I'm pretty sure something died in the chimney. But before you go, listen to my offer."

I paused.

"I'm willing to take an even split," she said. "The four of us work together, and once we find the treasure, we can each claim twenty-five percent of the reward. You can't get any fairer than that."

She was right. It did sound like a fair offer, which, coming from Raven, made me immediately suspicious.

I slowly sat down, hoping I wouldn't regret it. "What's the catch? As long as I've known you, you've never made an offer that wasn't in your favor."

Raven laughed. "I've never had to because I always knew that even if you found a treasure before me, I could take it away from you. But I've been thinking about that message. Whoever sent it made perfectly clear that the treasure only goes to whoever finds it first. There is a small possibility that if you get there before me, I won't be allowed to steal it. But with the four of us working together, everybody wins."

"What about Klart?"

"Forget about him. He's probably home playing video games by now." Raven stood up. "You can't make everyone happy, Gray. The people who arranged this competition know that. It's why they put the *I* inside of an eye. You have to look out for yourself first."

"That's the difference between us," I said. "I try to help other people by sharing what I find. All you care about is making sure you're on the side that wins."

Raven snorted and turned to Maya and Jack. "What about the two of you? Maya, you're clearly the brains of the operation, and nobody can get in and out of tricky situations better than Jack. Not to mention those night vision goggles of his could come in handy."

Jack tapped the goggles he'd pushed up on his head and beamed.

"Aren't you sick of Graysen giving away the treasures you help him find?" Raven asked. "If you join me, I guarantee you'll each get a third."

Maya folded her arms. "How do we know you won't double-cross us?"

"You don't," Raven said. "But the two of you will have me outnumbered. And if it comes down to a footrace at the end, your brother's way faster than I am. Together, we'll be unbeatable."

Jack whispered to Maya, and she nodded. "We saw how you treated the second-grade spies when they helped you. No deal."

I couldn't have been prouder of the two of them if I'd taught them about treasure hunting myself—which I kind of had. "Face it, Red Raven. Being selfish isn't ever going to bring you anything but sorrow."

Raven sneered. "We'll see who's sorry when I find the treasure first and the three of you end up empty-handed. Again."

"I'd rather come in last and keep my dignity," Maya said, "than come in first by cheating."

"But it's even better to come in first without cheating," Jack's voice said from the shadows of a pillar he'd slipped behind. His night vision goggles shifted in the darkness. "Then you get to keep your dignity *and* all the Legos."

CHAPTER 10
His Eyes Ring a Bell

"Nothing makes a man so adventurous as nothing in his pocket." That's either an idea from The Hunchback of Notre Dame or a thing Jack said when he forgot his lunch money. Either way, it makes a lot of sense.

"What now?" Maya asked as the three of us walked out of the girls' bathroom. "Do you think Raven was asking to join us because she doesn't know where to start looking?"

"Raven always has a plan. That's what makes her so hard to beat." I rubbed my chin. "Whoever sent us on this hunt didn't give us an obvious place to start. That means they either expected us to know where to begin the search, or they gave us a clue we just haven't noticed yet."

Jack pushed his night vision goggles back up on his head and scratched his nose before whispering to his sister.

"Could it be something about the spelling bee medal?" Maya translated.

"I hope not, or we're in big trouble," I said. The good

news was that if the clue was on the medal, at least Raven wouldn't know where to look either.

Walking down the school hall, I glanced at the decorations in each of the classrooms. The kindergarteners had been busy making werewolf heads out of brown felt and pipe cleaners. The first graders had hung dozens of bats from the ceiling with clear plastic fishing line, while the second-grade desks and walls were filled with construction paper spiders. Even though I knew the spiders weren't real, I kept my distance from the long legs and pointed fangs.

Maya thought for a minute. "What if the first clue was hidden in the *message*?"

I tapped the side of my head. The kid was catching on fast. "Nice thinking. We all saw it at the same time, so the start of the hunt would be fair. And it would be easy to camouflage a clue among the letters or even in the specific words they chose. Classic cryptography."

"You already figured it out, didn't you?" Maya asked. "That's why you didn't agree to join Raven."

"Afraid not. I spent the last two hours of class trying to crack the code. But the best I could come up with is that the first letters of each word can spell, 'Gasp. Spooky Dutch attic bib by pasta pathway gift spy.' Does that mean anything to the two of you?"

Jack wrinkled his nose.

"I know," I said. "Besides there are still a lot of random letters left over."

"So you've got nothing?" Maya blew a strand of hair out of her face.

"Pretty much," I admitted, wondering what I'd missed.

Maya stopped halfway down the hall and pointed. "What about that?"

Turning, I saw that Raven had been true to her word. Hanging on the door to the twins' classroom was the portrait of Howard Sullivan III.

Could it really be that simple? Had the clue been staring us in the face from the beginning? If the computer message and spelling bee medal were both the work of one person, it made sense that the clue would be hidden somewhere in the first thing we found.

"You're a genius," I said.

Maya scrunched up her face. "Be careful with the compliments or I might start expecting them."

"Sorry." I laughed. "It won't happen again."

I splashed water from a nearby drinking fountain onto my face to put me back in the game, then approached the painting the way I would a puzzle or a trap. Surrounded by paper pumpkins and bats, it looked even creepier than it had under the stage.

Running my fingers along the edge of the frame, I found something that looked like it could be a button, but it ended up just being a knot in the wood. I'd already looked at the back of the canvas when we first found it, but I lifted the painting to check again. There wasn't anything there unless a message was written in invisible ink or was only visible under certain types of light.

Using a magnifying glass from my archaeology kit, I studied the portrait itself. It was painted in oil, the brush-strokes harsh and angled, making the stern face appear even more serious.

"What are you looking for?" Maya asked.

"I'm not sure," I said. "Anything out of the ordinary. Odd shapes or colors that don't quite blend."

Maya shuddered. "All I see is a freaky old man. His eyes follow me wherever I go like he's about to chop me up."

"All the internet articles described him as being very generous and kind," I said. "There was nothing about him being a secret axe murderer."

Jack stared up into the wrinkled old face, bobbing his head left and right and up and down. Finally, he shivered and pulled his goggles back on.

"It's just an optical illusion," I said. "The artist painted him staring straight ahead. But because the surface of the canvas is flat, he seems to be looking at you no matter what angle you view him from."

"Do you think there's a message hidden under the paint?" Maya asked, running her fingers across its surface.

"I hope not," I said. "I'd hate to destroy something with this kind of historical significance."

Jack whispered to his twin.

"He says he can use crayons to fix anything you mess up."

"I'll keep that in mind."

Putting away the magnifying glass, I stepped back to take in the entire image. "Hold on. Something doesn't make sense. Look at the school doors behind him."

Maya and Jack studied the painting. "They're tilted," Maya said.

"Or *he* is," I muttered, tilting my head to get a better look.

Maya sucked at her lower lip. "But he's looking straight out. You said that's why his eyes follow you."

I nodded. "Right. The only way that would work is if the person who painted him was standing across from the school entrance somewhere above him and to the left."

Jack whispered, and Maya shook her head.

"I have no idea why the painter would be standing on the roof of Mrs. Ogleby's house."

Mrs. Ogleby was an old lady with about a hundred cats who lived in a two-story house across the street from the school. When it was hot, she let kids play in her front yard sprinklers as they walked home.

"Mrs. Ogleby's house wasn't there a hundred years ago," I said, trying to form a map in my head. "And that's not where the school entrance used to be. Before Principal Redbeard left and they replaced the old section, the entrance was back by where the soccer field is now. If you stood outside while raising your head up and to the left, you might be able to figure out whatever he was looking at."

Together, we all ran out the back door of the school, dodging around people setting up tents and games while keeping Jack away from the cotton candy booth.

When we reached the edge of the field, Jack and Maya titled their heads up and to the side the way the man in the painting had. I didn't have to. I could already tell what they were looking at.

"The bell tower," I whispered.

Back when Ordinary Elementary was first built, a large brass bell rang every morning at the start of school and every afternoon when school got out. The bell had been replaced by an intercom system before any of us were born, but the bell was still there in a wooden tower that rose from the roof on the second story of the building. No one used it anymore except for special occasions. But there was no question that was where the man in the portrait was looking.

Maya held a hand above her eyes, squinting at the small tower with a pointed roof and white wooden rails. "Wouldn't the artist have to be standing all the way up there to get the angle right?"

"It seems like it," I said. "Maybe the bell was one of the things Mr. Sullivan paid for."

Maya jumped up and down. "Maybe there is a clue hidden in the bell."

"Maybe," I said. "But they always keep the door to the bell tower locked, and it's impossible to—"

I stopped talking as a figure appeared on the first-floor roof of the newer section of the school, glanced quickly around, then shimmied up a drainpipe to the second level. From there, they scurried up to the tower and climbed over the railing before disappearing inside.

"Raven," I growled. "How did she figure that out?"

"No, look!" Maya pointed back up to the tower, where the figure was waving down at us. This time, I spotted the goggles on top of his head.

I spun around. "Jack?"

Maya shrugged. "I didn't even see him leave."

Jack pointed into the tower and pretended to open a door.

"Come on," I said. "Let's get up there before he decides to try ringing the bell."

CHAPTER 11
The Bell Tower

It is a truth universally acknowledged that a kid in possession of something that makes their voice echo will immediately start yelling into it.

When Maya and I had opened the door Jack had unlocked from the inside and started climbing the narrow staircase up to the bell tower, we could hear Jack's echoing voice above us.

"Ladies-adies-adies and gentlemen-en-en, welcome-welcome-welcome to the fight of the century-ry-ry. Spider-Man-an-an versus unicorn Godzilla-illa-illa."

At the top of the stairs, I saw him standing under the bell with his head hidden inside.

"What are you doing?" I asked. "This is supposed to be a top secret mission."

"Sorry-orry-orry." He ducked his head and scrambled out.

Joining him inside the tower, I could see that no one had been up there for a while. The thick carpet of dust on the wooden floor was broken only by Jack's footprints, and

there were cobwebs everywhere, including in Jack's hair.

The bell itself didn't seem like
anything special. The metal was
green with tarnish and the rope
looked like something had been
gnawing on it. Watching for spiders, I ducked under the edge and peeked
inside. It just looked like the inside of an
old bell.

Maya rubbed her nose and sneezed.
"At least we know we're the first ones to figure out the clue."

"Or there's no clue here at all." I kicked a splintery
board. "This bell has been here for as long as the school has.
If there was a clue here, don't you think someone would
have found it by now?"

Maya jutted out her chin. "No one knew about the
stairs hidden under the girls' bathroom until we found the
cafeteria menu. And the laminated hall pass on top of Desk
Mountain would still be lost if you hadn't discovered that
girl's note. You can't always see clues right away."

"Fair point," I said. "I guess I'm just feeling a little dis-
couraged. Let's try again. Look for anything that doesn't
seem like it should be there—words, buttons, symbols."

Jack handed me his night vision goggles.

"Be careful with those," Maya said. "He never lets anyone else use them."

"Thanks," I said, trying not to get choked up by my friend's trust. "But I'm really not sure how these would—"

Jack whispered something to Maya.

"He says there are letters written on the inside of the bell, but it's too dark inside to see them without the goggles."

"What?" I pulled on the night vision goggles and ducked under the bell, nearly knocking myself out when my head hit the metal with a dull *bong-ong-ong*.

"Do that again," Jack said from outside the bell. "It was really funny."

"Maybe to you, but—" I paused. "Wait, how are you talking out loud when it's still light?"

"No one can see me except Maya," Jack said.

"Good point." I rubbed the back of my head, where a bump was forming. But I forgot all about it when I saw the letters Jack was talking about.

Engraved into the metal, they'd been all but invisible before. But with Jack's goggles amplifying the light coming from outside, they jumped right out at me.

"Strange," I said, running my fingers over them. "Most of the metal inside the bell is as tarnished as the outside, but the area around the letters is only a little greenish, like somebody cleaned it off in the last few years."

"Who cares," Maya said. "What do they say?"

"Right." Swiveling my head to take in the whole thing, I read, "*Education is the key to unlock the golden door to freedom. George Washington Carver, 1896.*"

"The key to the golden door!" Maya shouted, her voice echoing inside the bell. "That has to be a clue."

"Do you want me to ring the bell now?" Jack asked.

"No!" Maya and I said at the same time.

Turning around, I spotted something else on the other side. "There are stars too," I said, counting them quickly. "Seven of them."

Outside the bell, Jack gasped. "Just like the symbol on the back of the spelling bee medal."

"We're definitely in the right place," Maya said, bouncing up and down.

After checking the rest of the bell, I crouched low and stepped outside.

"Were there any spiders in there?" Maya asked.

"Why?" I quickly dusted off my fedora, checking my hair and back for sticky webs. "Do you see something?"

"No," she said with a grin. "Just curious."

Third graders were the worst.

I gave Jack his goggles and ran my hands over the outside of the bell to see if there might be etching there as well, but I only felt smooth metal.

"Maybe we *should* ring it," Maya said. "There doesn't seem to be anything else to try."

"No," I repeated as Jack reached for the rope. "The minute we pull that, a dozen teachers will be up here to make us come down."

Maya thought for a moment. "What if there's a specific

pattern? Like the way we had to move the bathroom tiles to open the secret passage."

Jack whispered, and she nodded excitedly. "Yes! Seven times for the seven stars."

Jack lunged for the rope again, and I barely managed to hold him back. "That's not a bad idea. But we have to be sure before we try. We'll only get one chance."

I stared down at the people setting up the carnival rides, still amazed that the Ferris wheel, roller coasters, and other tents were all part of our little school carnival. All it would take was for one of the workers to spot kids in the tower and all three of us would be facing another detention like—

"The road in front of the school looks like the shape on the back of the star," Maya said.

"What?" I turned around to where the twins were looking down at the front of the school. Earlier, the road and the curved lane in front of the school's entrance would have been full of cars picking kids up, but now they were almost empty.

"If you pretend the roads are lines," Maya said, tracing the shape of the straight road in front of the school and the curved pickup lane with her finger, "it looks like a capital D turned on its side, or the protractor shape on the symbol."

It took me a moment to get what she was saying. When it did, I rubbed my hand across my mouth, trying to decide if we were really seeing what we thought we were or if it was just our imaginations.

I pulled out my field journal and opened it to the page where I'd copied the symbol from Howard Sullivan's ring.

Jack, who had found a package of ranch-flavored corn nuts I kept in my pack for emergencies, tapped the seven stars above it, leaving a trail of corn nut crumbs on the page.

"Just like the stars inside the bell," Maya said.

"Exactly. Except they're turned the wrong way. In order for them to match the curve of the road, they'd have to be . . ." My words died away as I turned to look at the bell. "Grab the edges."

Maya's eyes lit up. "You want us to turn it to match the stars on the symbol!"

"If we can," I said. Normal bells don't turn, but this

seemed too perfect to be a coincidence. "Be careful not to move it sideways. We don't want to accidentally make it ring."

Even with all three of us pulling, nothing happened at first. Then, creaking and grinding, the bell slowly rotated.

When it looked about right, Jack ducked inside. "A little more," he said. "More. Three more inches. And . . . *stop.*" A second later, he popped out.

"Was something supposed to happen?" Maya asked, wiping sweat from her face.

I looked at Jack. "Are you sure it's lined up right?"

He held his arm out in front of him and lined it up with the road, ducked under the bell, then came out with two thumbs up.

"Let's think about this," I said. "There wasn't any kind of click. Maybe we turned it the wrong way. Or maybe there's something else we have to do. Push a button or pull a—"

Before I could stop him, Jack grabbed the bell rope with both hands, braced his feet against the floor, and gave it an enormous tug, breaking the sound of the workers below with a startlingly loud *BONG*!

For a second, Maya and I could only stare at each other in shock. Then the floor swung open under our feet, and we all plummeted into the darkness like pieces of candy dropping into the chute of a gumball machine.

CHAPTER 12
The Card Catalog

If an alligator is nearby but no one
except Jack can see it, does it really exist?
We will probably never know.

"Maya? Jack? Are you two okay?" I asked, pushing myself up from the cold, mossy smelling water that splashed around my knees once I was standing. It was so dark I couldn't see either of them. I could barely make out the shape of my hand when I waved it in front of my face.

"I think so," Maya said, coughing. "But I accidentally got some of that water in my mouth, and it tastes like old shoes and dead fish."

Not an appetizing combination.

"I'm great," Jack said. "That was awesome. Can we do it again?"

"I'd rather not." After falling through the floor of the bell tower, the three of us had tumbled down a curving metal slide before landing here. I shook my sopping fedora and pushed my dripping hair out of my eyes. But I still couldn't see a thing.

I reached down, trying to find my pack that had fallen off on the slide. But all I could feel was warm, dank water with odd lumps floating on the top and some sort of hard, slimy floor at the bottom.

"Are you looking for this?" Jack asked, pushing my pack into my arms. Amazingly, it was still dry. "I saw it falling down the slide with us and grabbed it before we fell into the water."

"How did you—" I started, before remembering about his night vision googles. "You can see?"

"Perfectly," he said.

Maya coughed. "Where are we?"

"It looks like the kind of swimming pool they have at some gyms," Jack said.

Maya coughed again, taking a splashing step toward me. "Does our school have a swimming pool?"

"It used to a long time ago," I said. "But I thought they tore it out." I unzipped my pack and found my flashlight. "Let me just turn on a light and—"

"I wouldn't do that right now," Jack said, his clammy hand touching my arm.

I paused, my finger on the button. "Why not?"

"First, because I don't think it would be a good idea for my sister to see what she got in her mouth," Jack said. "It might make her barf."

"Gross." Maya gagged. "Now I *am* going to barf."

"Sorry about that," Jack said. "But mostly, I wouldn't turn it on because it might attract the alligators."

The flashlight in my hand suddenly felt as heavy as a stack of new textbooks. "The *what*?"

"Alligators," Jack said as calmly as if he were describing a TV show he'd just seen. "Right now, they're watching us from the other end of the pool. But if you turn on your light they could come closer to explore, and I probably taste like corn nuts."

For a moment, we were all completely silent. Then Maya spoke, her words high and trembling. "Are you sure there are alligators down here, Jack? This isn't just one of your stories, like the time you said a clown from Pete's Pizza Palace followed you home and was living under your bed?"

Jack snorted. "That wasn't a story. A clown did follow me home from Pete's Pizza Palace, and it did live under my bed until I forced it out by surrounding it with stinky socks."

I took a deep breath. "But you are 100 percent sure there are real, honest-to-goodness alligators down here in the water with us right now?"

"Well . . ." Jack paused, and I could hear the water churning as he moved to get a better view. "They look like alligators. But I guess they could just be scaly poodles with big teeth. Or giant killer tree frogs with long noses. Or

possibly crocodiles. I don't really know the difference. But we should know for sure in a minute because they're heading our way."

Something snapped in the dark, and I could swear the water around me rippled.

"Do something!" Maya shouted.

Throwing my backpack over one arm, I spun around in the darkness to see what was coming toward us, but it was like trying to play a game of Pin the Tail on the Donkey where you were still dizzy and blindfolded, only the donkey was coming to eat you.

"Which way do we go to get out of here?" I called.

"Hmm," Jack said. "I can see a set of stairs. But it looks like they're blocked by a bunch of broken cement. And there's a door on the other side, but it's boarded over."

"Stop telling us ways we can't get out and tell us a way we can!" Maya shouted.

Something splashed nearby.

"What about a ladder?" I asked. "Pools always have those."

"No ladders," Jack said, still sounding surprisingly calm. "But there are a whole bunch of teeny tiny dresser drawers."

I rubbed my ears, wondering if I'd heard him wrong. "Dresser drawers?"

"That's what they look like," Jack said. "There's a huge stack of them piled up at the end of the pool. Only the drawers are really small. Like the size rabbits would keep their sweatshirts in. If rabbits wore sweatshirts. Only instead of having clothes in them, the ones that are open are filled with little pieces of—"

"I don't care what they're filled with," Maya yelled. "If we can climb them, take us there before we get eaten."

"That's probably a good idea," Jack said, grabbing my hand. "The big-toothed poodles are really close, and they look hungry."

"Hurry," Maya yelled, and I guessed Jack must be leading her with his other hand because I could hear them both splashing next to me.

"Here," Jack said as I slammed into something hard.

Reaching out, I could feel pretty much what Jack had described—square wooden drawers with small metal handles. I tried to pull one open, but it wouldn't move.

"They're stuck," Maya shouted, and something growled in the water behind us.

Jack's voice came from somewhere above me. "Some of them are open. You can use them like steps to climb up."

Moving to my left, I banged my shin on what I guessed was an open drawer. At the same time, I reached above me and felt another open drawer a few feet higher and to the side. They each felt about six inches wide and more than long enough to stand on. Stepping from one drawer to another while grabbing the ones above me, I pulled myself out of the water.

"I'm climbing," I called.

"Watch your feet," Jack yelled, and something crunched

just below me as a puff of hot, humid air that smelled liked rotting turtles spread over me.

I reached up in the darkness and was pulling myself from one drawer to another when, without any warning, one of them broke loose from the cabinet above me. At the same time, a shoe slammed into my right eye.

"Sorry," Jack said. "One of the drawers I was holding broke."

"Me too," Maya said. "It's like some of them are barely attached."

"Hold on," I shouted, my face still smarting. "This could be a test. Both of you stop moving."

Careful to keep a firm hold on a drawer with my right hand, I reached into my backpack with my left, grabbed my flashlight, and pushed the button.

"Ouch," Jack shouted. "A little warning before—" His words cut off as I shined the light to find him pushing up his night vision goggles.

"Sorry," I said, moving the beam over to where Maya was clinging to shelves a few feet away from me. "Are you okay?"

"I think so," she said. "At least for now."

I moved my light down to the murky green liquid, which was every bit as disgusting as Jack had suggested. He was right. It did seem to be a large rectangular pool. Swinging my light to one side, I could see the remains of a broken diving board. The rusty handle of a pool sweeper jutted up out of stagnant water filled with greasy green moss, floating oily patches, and strands of sickly yellow vegetation.

Every now and then, large brown bubbles rose from the water and burst with a disgusting *splat*!

Clinging to the shelves on my right, Maya gagged.

"Told you," Jack called from above my head.

"I don't see any alligators," I said, scanning the water.

"They swam back under when we started climbing," he said cheerfully. "I can go back down and get them, though, if you want."

"No," Maya said at once.

Above the pool, a row of rusty metal beams was bolted to a concrete ceiling.

"We must be somewhere under the school," I said.

"How do we get out?" Maya asked.

The stairs Jack had mentioned were filled with mounds of construction debris—definitely not climbable. There were metal doors on each side of the pool, but both of them were boarded over and the sides of the pool had caved in, making it impossible to reach either of them without going back into the water.

"It looks like the only way out is up," I said just as a gushing sound came from somewhere over our heads. A blast of brown-tinted water nearly knocked me off my hold, but I grabbed a shelf to my left and swung away.

"What is this we're climbing?" Maya asked, wiping a hand across her mouth.

I scanned my light up the rows of small wooden drawers with curved brass handles and moldy cardboard cards tucked into metal frames on the front. Long green vines with tiny white flowers wove up through some of the handles.

"I've never actually used one," I said. "But I'm pretty sure we're climbing the world's biggest card catalog."

"Pokémon cards?" Jack shouted excitedly. "This thing could be worth millions."

"Not Pokémon cards," I said. "Library cards. In ancient times before people had cell phones, or computers, or any of the really cool stuff we have, to find a book in a library, you had to look up the author or subject on these little paper cards and locate something called the Dewey decimal number to find it in the shelves."

Above us, water rushed again.

"Look out!" I shouted as another brownish mini-waterfall splashed down toward Maya. Scrambling to her right, she ducked under a shelf that broke away the minute the water poured over it.

Pointing my light up, I spotted an ancient-looking drinking fountain—its metal case filled with large rusty holes and patches of furry white moss. "Looks like that's what's keeping the pool filled."

"Let's see what's at the top," Jack said, climbing happily up a few more shelves.

"Wait!" I called just as the next shelf he grabbed broke free and dropped into the pool below us with a splash.

"Why do they keep doing that?" Maya cried.

"Let me test a theory," I said.

The waterlogged card on the front of the drawer I was

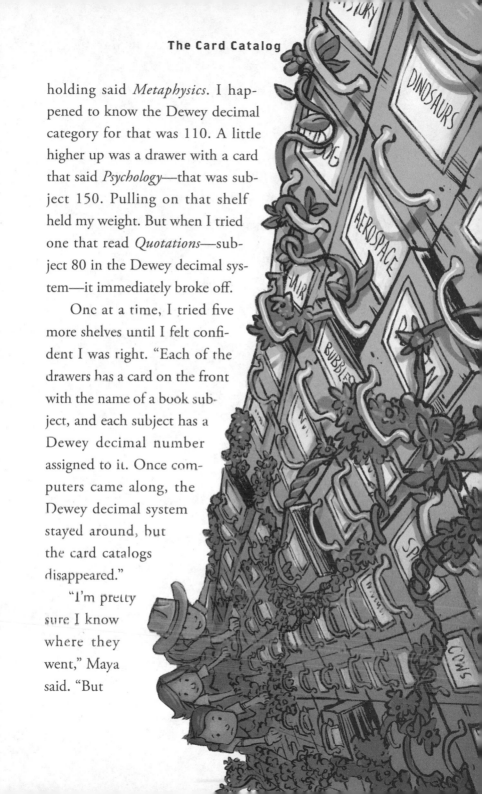

holding said *Metaphysics*. I happened to know the Dewey decimal category for that was 110. A little higher up was a drawer with a card that said *Psychology*—that was subject 150. Pulling on that shelf held my weight. But when I tried one that read *Quotations*—subject 80 in the Dewey decimal system—it immediately broke off.

Once at a time, I tried five more shelves until I felt confident I was right. "Each of the drawers has a card on the front with the name of a book subject, and each subject has a Dewey decimal number assigned to it. Once computers came along, the Dewey decimal system stayed around, but the card catalogs disappeared."

"I'm pretty sure I know where they went," Maya said. "But

skip the library class and tell us why some of them are broken."

"I don't think they are," I said. "The drawers that have higher subject numbers than the ones below them stay attached. But the ones with lower numbers break off."

Maya's eyes got as big and round as the playground spinner at recess. "You're saying this is part of the test?"

"Pretty sure," I said. "The key is finding subjects with a higher and higher number until we finally reach the top."

It was tricky, but not nearly the worst trap I'd faced.

"Follow me," I called. "My years of being a research nerd are finally going to pay off."

CHAPTER 13

The Math Room

When I told my math teacher that my life would never depend on whether I could solve word problems . . . I was wrong.

"If this really is still part of the treasure hunt, it's the worst one ever," Maya gasped as I pulled her over the top of the last card catalog drawer where dim light buzzed from a pair of neon bulbs in the ceiling.

We both collapsed onto the floor of a hallway with warped yellow tiles and cinderblock walls covered with faded paint that might once have been mint green. "I mean, we've survived traps and solved puzzles before, but what kind of monster leaves clues that can only be solved by someone odd enough to have the Dewey decimal system memorized?"

I wanted to be offended, but I was too tired.

"I wouldn't do that," Maya called to Jack, who was about to take a gulp from the large rusty drinking fountain at the top of the card catalog.

Maya pointed to a sign that read *Drinking Fountain of Youth.*" She looked back at me. "You don't think that's really . . . ?"

"I don't know," I said. "But I wouldn't take a chance on wearing diapers and going through potty training all over again."

Jack quickly backed away from the fountain, wiping the back of his hand across his lips.

"What do you really think the treasure at the end is?" Maya asked, sitting beside me. "I mean, we're not looking for a bunch of toys someone took, and we're definitely not searching for a laminated hall pass—which you still haven't let me borrow, by the way."

"Just let me know when you need it," I said, patting my pack.

I had to admit I wasn't sure what we were on the trail of. I'd searched for plenty of valuable items in my time—The Hankie of Harold, rumored to cure any cold; a four square ball that had won 2,349 straight games before rolling down a haunted sewer grate; a pair of missing basketball high-top shoes Laurie Winkle swore made you leap seventeen inches higher than your highest jump. But what we were after now felt bigger than any of those.

"It has to be valuable if someone went to this much trouble to hide it," I said. "But there's something else. If

you combine a spelling bee medal, translating a phrase from Phoenician into Latin into English, a quote about the importance of education, and a trap that requires a detailed knowledge of library science, what do you get?"

Jack whispered to Maya.

"Someone who wears bowties and knows the answer to every trivia question?" Maya asked.

"Maybe," I said, not admitting that I had a large collection of bowties in my closet. "But add the motto *Intelligence over all* and you also get someone who's trying to test how smart we are."

"Or at least if we're smart in the ways they want us to be," Maya said. "What kind of treasure do you give a supersmart kid, anyway? A bumper sticker that says *I Get Better Grades than You?*"

"Good question," I said. "I usually don't think much about what I might get. I just want to figure out what it is and how it got there. It's like the knowledge is its own reward."

"Hmm." Maya nodded. "I guess I don't care about getting the treasure that much either. But it would be great to find something so amazing everyone would know about it. There aren't enough famous women treasure hunters."

"Well, there's one way to find out for sure," I said. The three of us walked down the hallway that—not surprisingly—was bricked closed less than a dozen feet in. On one side of the hall, a few feet before the bricks, was a closed door with a pitted metal sign that read *Math Room*.

Maya groaned. "You don't happen to be a math whiz too, do you?"

"Sorry," I said. "Just thinking about fractions makes me dizzy. What about you two?"

Maya and Jack looked at each other. "We're okay," Maya said. "But do you really think whatever puzzle they have in there is going to use third-grade math?"

"It might not be too bad," I said. "It's got to be better than going back the way we came."

But the minute we stepped inside, I was pretty sure I was wrong. Unlike most classrooms, the room on the other side of the door had eight perfectly equal walls, including the side we entered through, and a wall with a large metal grate in the middle directly across from us.

The other six walls had a table and chair set beneath a numbered whiteboard with a math problem written in the middle. Instead of desks, the center of the room was piled high with a huge stack of math books, calculators, pencils, slide rules, compasses, and a strange box filled with wooden rods covered by numbers and symbols. I picked up one of the books from the pile and frowned. "Trigonometry?"

"Definitely not third grade," Maya said. "This is the octagon of my nightmares. Or is an eight-sided shape called a heptagon?"

I shook my head.

"You don't know?" She scowled. "Don't they teach you that kind of stuff in fifth grade?"

"Probably," I said. "But I'm a man of history, not

mathematics." When they just looked at me, I admitted, "Okay, I'm really bad at math."

Jack bolted for the exit, but just as he reached it, the door slammed shut. He tugged desperately at the knob, but it wouldn't budge.

"Locked," I muttered. "I probably should have seen that coming."

Maya pounded on the thick wood and examined the knob before shaking her head. "Even if Jack had his tools, there isn't a lock to pick."

I crossed the room and peered through the grate where a set of old mine cart rails disappeared down a steep incline. The metal bars were too thick to cut or bend. My trusty elastic sticky hand could fit between them, but there didn't appear to be any kind of switch or lever on the other side to open the grate.

Jack whispered to Maya.

"I don't know how we can still be in the school," she said. "I can accept a hidden pool and a stack of old library card catalogs. But I'm pretty sure if we had a mine, I would have heard about it."

"It looks like the only way out is solving the puzzles," I said miserably. "We might as well check them out. Let's start at number one."

Taking a calculator from the pile, I approached the whiteboard with a number one above it and read the problem.

Eight who ate at eight await,
There to sate with knife and plate

A thousand meals well deserved,
Add eight of eight they shall be served.

Maya shook her head. "I'm almost positive that's not part of the third-grade curriculum."

"I don't think it's part of any curriculum," I said. "It sounds like something from one of those cooking shows where British people try to make cakes out of pudding, toffee, and baking soda."

I studied the symbols on the calculator, but there didn't seem to be anything about feeding a thousand people at eight or any other time.

Jack put his hands to Maya's ear, whispering furiously as he pointed at me, the doors, Maya, the pile of math books, the problems on the walls, my backpack, and finally the bottom of one of his shoes.

"Well?" I asked when he was finally finished. "Does he have a plan?"

Maya rolled her eyes. "He thinks you should guess."

That sounded like a really bad idea, but maybe we'd get lucky. I took a deep breath. "Two hundred and thirty-one?"

Nothing happened.

I tried again a little louder. "The square root of seventeen."

Jack pointed to a marker lying on the table.

"Oh, right." I picked up the pen, thinking furiously. Sometimes when I wasn't sure of the right answer to a test question, I tried answering with something that could be interpreted a few different ways.

Grasping the pen in my sweaty fingers I wrote

A knife and plate are really great,
But most kids eat way before eight
So I would give them pretzel sticks
And squeezy cheese to eat at six.

The minute I set the pen back on the table, a light in the top corner of the whiteboard flashed red, and the ceiling lowered a few feet toward us with a thud. The entire room trembled.

"I don't think it appreciates creative answers," Maya said.

Jack said something to Maya, who shook her head.

"This isn't *Star Wars*, and we aren't inside a trash compactor." She looked around the room. "Let's find an easier problem."

Together we checked each of the walls. None of them looked any easier, and a couple were downright creepy—like the one that said we had to solve the problem using some guy's bones.

"I'm sorry," I said, dropping the calculator back onto the pile and sliding to the floor. I put my head in my hands. "I never should have made you come in here."

Maya sat in front of me and tipped up my fedora. "You didn't make us do anything. We came because we believe in you, and in ourselves."

Jack rubbed his thumb and fingers together.

"And because we wanted our share of the treasure."

"Well, it seems like both of those were bad ideas," I said.

"I don't know how to solve these problems, and it doesn't look like we're getting any treasure."

"Then I guess it's a good thing I showed up," said a familiar voice.

Jack, Maya, and I all looked around, but there was no one else in the room.

High up on the wall, an air vent grate jiggled and clanged to the floor. Raven poked her head out. "Hey, guys, miss me?"

After rolling down a slide, falling into a pool of disgusting water, nearly getting eaten by alligators, and climbing a killer card catalog, Maya, Jack, and I were a mess. But Raven looked even worse. Her cheeks were scratched and covered with grease, her hair looked like she'd been sucked backward into a vacuum, swirled around, and spit out again, her hands were filthy, a couple of her nails were chipped, and her clothes smelled like she'd been vomited on by a really large cat.

But she was grinning as she squirmed out of the vent, swung down, and dropped to the floor.

"Cool room," she said, hands on her hips. She looked over at the pile of calculators and math books. "What did you do, rob a math teacher?"

"How did you find us?" I asked, staring from her up to the grate. "And what is that all over you?"

"You don't want to know," she said. "But I got here using this."

She held out a crumpled file folder I recognized at once.

"The school plans "Let's Make a Deal" Larry tried to trade for the spelling bee medal. How did you get them?"

Raven rubbed her hands on her pants, tried to straighten her hair, then shrugged. "Everybody has a price. It turns out his was a mint condition Blastois Holo."

"A Pokémon," I said. I hadn't even thought about trying to trade for Larry's map once the medal got stolen.

Maya scratched her head. "That map told you how to find the treasure?"

"Not even close," Raven said. "I've been crawling around the vents for hours. You don't want to know how many abandoned rooms there are in this place. I think I found the mummified remains of a substitute teacher next to a jammed copy machine waiting for her word search sheets to finish printing."

She plucked a dust ball the size of a kitten off her shoulder. "The only reason I found my way here is because I heard your voices."

"Please tell me you're a math genius," I said. "Or we're all in a lot of trouble."

"I'm amazing at everything," Raven said. "Although I don't know if I'd call myself a genius."

Maya, Jack, and I groaned.

"I am," a second voice said, and another face—even dirtier than Raven's—peeked out from the air vent.

Raven spun around. "Klart?"

CHAPTER 14

A Big Mistake

Sometimes a treasure hunter learns more
from their mistakes than they do from
their successes. Usually what they learn
is to never make that mistake again.

"How did *you* get here?" I asked.

Klart squeezed his shoulders partway through the vent, twisting to get his arms free, and finally blew out a frustrated breath. "Could you give me a hand? I'm kind of stuck."

Raven glared up at him, hands on her hips. "You *followed* me."

"Actually," Klart said, resting his chin on the edge of the opening, "I followed *them*. Who knew there was a secret staircase under the girls' bathroom? That Adventurer's Club is way better than the Doodler's office."

"It's called an *Explorer's Guild*," I said. "And you're not allowed to go in unless you're a member."

"I didn't." Klart squirmed around again before giving up. "I mean, I wanted to. But then you guys started arguing, and I saw Gray and the twins turn around, so I ducked into one of the side tunnels."

Maya grimaced. "Bad idea. The side tunnels are a trap to keep out people who don't belong."

"You're telling me," Klart said. "I totally lost my sense of direction and ended up in a room where the only way to leave was by writing *I will not enter places where I don't belong* five hundred times on an enormous chalkboard. When I finally I got out, Raven was heading back to the stairs. So . . ."

"You spied on me when I was trading for Larry's maps and followed me into the vents!" Raven snapped.

Klart tried to shrug and only ended up getting more stuck. "You're the one who gave me the idea."

"Let's help him down," I said.

"Why?" Raven demanded. "He's just here for a share of the treasure."

Jack and Maya looked at each other. "We're *all* here for the treasure."

"I know that," Raven said. "But why should we give *him* any?"

"Because I know the answer to that math problem," Klart said. "It's actually not too bad when you think about it."

I looked back at the writing on the whiteboard. "The one about eating?"

"It's not really about eating," he said. "I mean, the story mentions food. But that's just a way of disguising a fairly simple math puzzle."

"Could have fooled me," I said, deciding I needed to pay more attention in math class.

Klart laughed. "The first hint is that there are eight 'eights' in the poem but spelled in different ways. Eight, ate, eight, aw*ait,* s*ate,* p*late,* eight, and eight. Then, in the last line it says you have to add eight of eight to serve a thousand meals."

I still didn't get it.

"The real question is in the numbers, and the answer is obvious when you think about it. Just add eight eights to total a thousand."

"Nice try," Raven said. "But eight eights added together only equal sixty-four."

Maya nodded.

"That all depends on how you add them," Klart said. "The largest number less than a thousand that you can form with only eights is eight hundred and eighty-eight. That still leaves one hundred and twelve. Add eighty-eight, and you have nine hundred and seventy-six. Three more eights give you twenty-four, and there you go. One thousand."

When he explained it that way, it did seem pretty easy.

I erased the answer I'd written and replaced it with

$$888 + 88 + 8 + 8 + 8 = 1000$$

This time the light on the whiteboard flashed green, and something clanged on the other side of the grate.

Jack and Maya ran to look through the bars, which were still shut tight.

"There's a cart on the tracks now," Maya said.

"A mine cart?" Raven asked.

"Not exactly. It looks more like the kind of cart teachers use to move things around the school."

The four of us pressed our faces against the bars to stare at a rickety metal cart balanced perfectly on the rails.

"What's that on top of it?" I asked, peering into the dark tunnel.

Jack put on his night vision goggles and whispered to Maya.

"He says it's a projector," Maya said.

As we watched, a set of chains in an opening next to the tracks began to move, and a rusty elevator sent a second cart rolling onto the tracks. As the two carts clanged together, a car battery on the bottom shelf of each cart sparked. The projectors turned on, sending an eerie green glow across the walls of the tunnel.

"What's going on over there?" Klart shouted.

Raven leaned down. "It looks like they replaced the wheels to fit the rails."

"But why would they put projector carts on mine tracks?" I asked.

Maya pointed into the tunnel to where the tracks disappeared in a terrifyingly steep drop. "You don't think we're supposed to ride them down the . . ."

"It doesn't seem very safe," I said.

Raven snickered. "Scared?"

My throat suddenly felt very dry.

"Stay here if you want," Raven said. "But if that's where the treasure is, I'm going."

"You can't open the grate unless you solve the math problems," Klart said. "And I won't help unless you get me down from here."

Raven turned and crossed the room, her eyes narrowed. "We'll let you down. But you only get ten percent of the treasure while the four of us each get twenty-three percent."

Klart snorted. "That adds up to 103 percent, which just proves you need me to get out of this room. We each get twenty percent."

"Okay," I said, ignoring Raven's glare. "But we all make a solemn adventures' promise that from here on out, we either find the treasure together or not at all."

"Deal," Klart said.

Maya whispered to Jack, and he nodded. "We agree too," she said.

Raven scowled. "Fine. But one of these days, I really need to teach you three about the power of negotiation."

I unsnapped the pouch on my belt and surveyed the situation. A single flick sent my elastic hand flying through the air. It hit dead center on Klart's forehead and stuck with a satisfying *splat*. "Hold on," I said, pulling.

"To what?" he squawked as he slid forward.

Klart must have been part cat, because the minute he was free of the vent, he managed to perform an impressive summersault, catapulting directly into the center of the

room. He crashed into the pile of calculators, his eyes wide, arms and legs flailing.

"Way to stick the landing," Raven said.

Jack whispered to his sister.

"It *was* funny," she agreed. "But I don't
think we can talk him into doing it again,
even if you missed the last part."

"Are you okay?" I asked, helping Klart up.

"Better than I was up there." He wiggled the toes of his
shoes. They looked like they'd gotten caught in the spokes of
a bike. "Something in there kept biting my feet."

"Well," Raven asked. "Are you going to solve those math
problems or stand around complaining?"

Klart shook his head. "Compared to you, the Doodler
is a marshmallow."

Raven shrugged. "Maybe that's why he spends his time
drawing pictures in a closet."

Klart didn't answer, too busy starting in on the remaining math problems. He solved the next three without even
checking his answers on a calculator.

The fifth one made him scratch his chin.

Half of a school takes calculus classes.
Three-fifths of those students wear braces or
     glasses.
Braces and glasses are equally split,
A third of the spectacled for braces are fit.
If you should wish to gain full satisfaction,

Express the percentage with both as a
fraction.
The smart will perceive the results in their
head.
The wise use the bones of a scholar long dead.

"Too hard for your genius brain?" Raven asked.

"It's not that," Klart said, but Raven was already pushing past him.

"I've got this." She stepped forward to write the answer and frowned. "Hey, where's the marker?"

Klart raised a finger. "Maybe there's a reason it's not on the table."

"Of course there is," she said. "Somebody must have swiped it."

Jack turned out his pants pockets to show he hadn't taken it while Raven grabbed a marker from another table and started writing. "Half of the school as a fraction is ½. If three-fifths of that half wear either glasses or braces, that's three-fifths times one half."

$$3/5 \times 1/2 = 3/10$$
$$30/100 = 30\%$$

Klart watched her work with a concerned expression, but when I looked at him, he only shrugged.

"If the number of students who wear glass or braces are evenly split, that means fifteen percent of the students wear glasses and fifteen percent wear braces. But this is where it gets tricky."

Raven held up the marker. "A third of the students who wear glasses also wear braces. And a third of fifteen percent equals five percent."

$$\frac{1}{2} \times 30\% = 15\%$$
$$\frac{1}{3} \times 15\% = 5\%$$

"But—" Klart tried to cut in.

"I know," Raven said. "I have to write it as a fraction." Leaning forward, she wrote:

$$\text{Answer} = \frac{1}{20}$$

Immediately, the room shook so hard it knocked us all to the floor and sent my hat flying. The top of the room plunged toward us, making the pile of math books and calculators spill everywhere.

"No!" I shouted, sure we were about to be crushed. But the ceiling stopped partway down, crumpling the top of the whiteboard's metal frame.

"What happened?" Raven asked, visibly shaken. She stared up at the ceiling. "The problem seemed so easy."

"That's what I was afraid of," Klart said. "It was *too* easy."

CHAPTER 15
The Last Question

Life is like Play-Doh. Get squeezed and
twisted enough, and you might just end
up looking like a kind of cool bird—even if
your beak is a little crooked and one of your
wings is slightly longer than the other.

"This is all my fault," Raven said, pacing around the now much-shorter room.

"Maybe not," Klart said.

"What are you talking about?" she asked. "I got the problem wrong."

"Except you didn't." Klart had to hunch his back to keep from hitting his head on the ceiling as he examined Raven's answer. "Your math is exactly right. On a test you would have received 100 percent—including full credit for showing your work."

Maya stood on her tiptoes and touched the ceiling. "Then why did the room almost smash us into pancakes?"

"You must have known something was wrong," Raven

said to Klart. "You tried to stop me from writing my answer."

"I had my suspicions. But the only thing I knew was that this problem was way easier than the others."

I picked up my hat from where it landed when I fell. "Maybe you did us all a favor. I mean, at least we know that getting the answer right isn't enough."

Raven clenched her jaw. "I don't need your pity."

"What are you talking about?" I asked.

"Admit I messed up," she growled.

I looked at Maya and Jack, who seemed as confused as I was. "Okay," I said. "You made a mistake."

"A mistake that was inexcusable." She clenched her fists, cheeks glowing red.

"I think you're being a little too hard on yourself," Klart said.

"I'm not," Raven snapped. "You tried to warn me, but I wouldn't listen. And do you know why I wouldn't?"

I looked at the others, hoping one of them would speak up. But they were all waiting for me. "Because you . . . thought you knew the answer?"

"No. The reason I didn't listen is that I wanted to prove how smart I was. To make you ask me to be the leader of the team instead of only letting me join you because I cheated and followed you." She ran her fingers through her hair, eyes glistening. "It's the same reason I installed the spyware on the school network. And why I took the painting. But this time, my arrogance could have killed us all."

I'd never seen Raven like this. "Obviously you're sorry. So let's just move on."

"I *am* sorry," she cried, dropping to the floor and burying her face in her hands. "But it's too late for apologies. I wanted to seem smart and powerful enough to lead you, but the truth is I don't deserve to be part of the team. Go on without me."

I didn't know what to say. Everything Raven had said was technically true—she didn't like to listen to anyone else. She was always trying to prove she was the smartest. And this wasn't the first time it had gotten other people into trouble. But that didn't mean she didn't deserve to come with us.

As I stood silently trying to figure out what to say, Klart crossed the room and sat on the floor beside her. "I lied when I said the only reason I helped pick on Graysen was because the Doodler made me."

"What are you saying?" I asked. This wasn't the way I'd imagined the treasure hunt going.

Klart glanced at me, then looked quickly away. "I did it because I kind of liked how it felt. Being the second-in-command to the most powerful kid at the school made me seem smart and important."

Raven gave a muffled grunt.

"I also lied about being in charge of the sixth graders while the Doodler is out sick," Klart said. "He fired me."

Raven rubbed her eyes and looked up. "Because you told him what he was doing was wrong?"

"No. Because I tried to do it myself." Klart laughed uneasily. "After Cameron and his friends embarrassed the Doodler, the rest of the sixth graders were talking about how weak he looked, and I saw my chance to be even more important. Why settle for second-in-command when I could run the Venerable but Quick-Tempered Order of the Sixth Graders myself?"

"That wasn't very nice," Maya said.

"It wasn't. But it turns out that being the Doodler's lieutenant didn't mean nearly as much as I thought I did. Nobody wanted me to be in charge. I was only playing games in the computer lab because the Doodler's henchmen were going to beat me up, and I was hiding from them."

"Why are you telling me this?" Raven asked.

Klart sighed. "Because I want you to know that we all make mistakes. And sometimes the reasons for those mistakes aren't very pretty. I mean, I can try to justify what I did. But the bottom-line truth is I chose to do the things I did, just like you chose to steal the painting from Gray and his friends and spy on emails."

He shifted so he was looking directly at her. "People make bad decisions because they think they'll look better, or it will make them powerful, or get them something they want. I did what I did, but looking back, I wish I hadn't. I've had more fun with you four today than I had the whole time I was helping the Doodler pick on other kids. I really hope it's not too late for you to apologize because if it is, that means it's too late for me as well. And I really want to try to do better."

He looked at me, Maya, and Jack. "When you shrimps get to be my age, try not to be mean to the kids who are younger than you."

Maya and Jack nodded, and I thought about what Klart had said. "I've made mistakes too," I said. "I should have gotten us to work together instead of going off on my own. I did it because I convinced myself I was the only one I could trust to find the treasure, but I never would have made it out of this room if it weren't for you two."

Raven sniffed, but I could see her trying to hide a hint of a smile. "We still might not get out."

"See," I said. "Even more proof of how bad I messed up. I'm sorry."

"I'm sorry for helping the Doodler bully you," Klart said.

I crossed the room and held my hand out to him. "It wasn't fun being picked on. But I believe you've changed, and I accept your apology."

"Thanks," Klart said, shaking my hand. "I'll try to make up for it by being a better person in the future. I accept your apology for making me almost get eaten in the air vents."

Klart turned to Raven and held out his hand. "I believe that you've changed, and I accept your apology for almost getting us smashed." He looked over at us. "Right?"

I nodded. "Definitely."

"Me too," Maya said. "You did bring the painting back, which is the only reason we found our way here."

"What?" Raven asked, looking over sharply.

"It's true," I said. "The painting was the first clue to finding the treasure. If you didn't give it back, we never would have discovered that someone had put a new bell in the tower."

Raven's eyes narrowed as she opened her mouth to speak, then shook her head. "I'm glad it helped."

"What about you?" Klart asked, looking at Jack. "Do you accept Raven's apology?"

Jack seemed to be considering asking for something in return, but after Maya elbowed him in the ribs, he quickly nodded.

"So what now?" Klart asked. "I'm guessing one more wrong answer and *phwutt!*" He clapped his hands together.

Jack and Maya looked at each other. "It might be time to go home," Maya said. "I mean, you three are old, but Jack and I still have a lot of our lives in front of us."

"I'm not sure that's an option anymore," I said, looking in the direction of the air vent Raven and Klart had climbed through. The opening was gone now, covered by the fallen ceiling, and the door Jack, Maya, and I had come through was locked. Despite our having solved four of the six puzzles, the grate hadn't opened at all. If we didn't solve the remaining problems, there was nowhere to go.

Raven got to her feet, trying to straighten her messy hair. "What do you want to do, Gray? I'll go along with whatever you decide."

"You will?" I asked.

She nodded. "You almost always do the right thing, and you've gotten us this far."

"Me too," Klart said.

Maya and Jack just smiled and nodded. I already knew they both had my back, but having everyone agree to follow my decision made me nervous. If it were just me, I would have pushed on. But how could I tell the others to take that risk?

"There might be someone watching us," I said, looking around the room for hidden cameras. "If we just wait here, they might show up to let us out."

"You want to give up the hunt?" Raven asked.

I shook my head. "Not really, but—"

"Trust your feelings," she said. "I believe you can get us out of here."

It was weird having Raven encourage me, but I kind of liked it.

I turned to Klart. "You said this math problem was easier than the others?"

"Way easier," he said. "The one with the eights wasn't very hard from a math standpoint. But the way it was written made it tricky. The next three were pretty advanced. Nothing they teach in elementary school. The only reason I knew the answers is because I'm a math geek. I expected the final two problems to be total brain busters, but this one was—"

"Easy *and* simple," I said. "Which probably means it's the hardest problem of all."

Jack frowned and whispered to Maya.

"I don't get it either," she said.

"It's like when you've been tracking a treasure for weeks," I said, "but when you finally reach it, it's sitting right out in the open. That's when you know you have to be careful, because the hardest traps to solve are the ones that don't appear to be traps at all."

I went back to study the question again, trying not to notice the way the ceiling had crumpled the top of the whiteboard it was written on. Even after Raven had solved it, I still didn't follow all of the percentages and fractions. But I could see what Klart meant when he said the problem was fairly clear.

Except for the last two lines.

"*The smart will perceive the results in their head.*" I turned to Raven. "You did this math problem in your head, right?"

She nodded.

"Because you're smart."

She grinned. "Thanks."

But what about the last line? "Klart, does *The wise use the bones of a scholar long dead* mean anything to you?"

"Not really," he said. "It sounds sort of gruesome. Like something you might read on a pirate map."

Jack whispered to Maya.

"No, I don't think we're going to have to draw straws to see whose bones we use."

"*Bones of a scholar long dead,*" I muttered. They were right. Solving a math problem with bones was disgusting.

Unless this was like the food problem, where the words were really talking about something else.

Wandering back across the room, I looked at the pile of math supplies. "Klart, did you use any of this stuff to solve the first four problems?"

He shook his head.

"Strange." I picked out one of the textbooks at random and flipped through its pages.

Maya tapped her foot. "Not sure now is the right time for a reading break."

She was probably right. It wasn't like I was going to make up for six years of bad homework habits by burying my nose in a bunch of advanced calculations now.

"No," Raven said as I started to put it back. "Graysen's right. Why would they leave all this stuff here if we didn't need it?" She walked to the pile and grabbed another book.

"Sounds good to me," Klart said, looking over the titles until he found one he liked.

Jack climbed up the pile, grabbed the book at the very top, and opened it, furrowing his brow as he turned the pages.

"Fine," Maya huffed, taking one for herself.

"Find anything?" Raven asked as I finished looking through my book and set it on a table in front of one of the problems we'd already finished.

"No," I said. "To be honest, I didn't even understand three-quarters of what was in there."

"Nice use of fractions," Klart said. "See, this room is helping you get better at math already."

"I don't see anything helpful in this one either," Raven said, placing her book on top of mine. "But I think we should keep looking."

"I'm always up for a math fest," Klart said, adding his book to the stack and taking two more.

For the next thirty minutes, the five of us worked our way through pages of theorems, expressions, quotients, and properties. As the stack of textbooks filled the first table and spread to a second, I started to wonder if the supplies had only been there as a distraction. Then Klart held up the book he was reading and shouted, "I've got it!"

"What did you find?" Raven asked.

"It's all right here in *Math through the Ages*," Klart said. He rushed back to the pile of supplies and pushed things around until he located the strange wooden box I'd noticed when we first came in. He set the open book and the box on the desk in front of the whiteboard.

"What is that?" I asked. I'd never seen anything like it.

On the left side of the box was a row of nine squares numbered one through nine going from the top to the bottom. Inside the box, ten rectangular wooden rods were set side by side. Each rod also had nine squares carved into it. The squares at the top of each rod contained a single number going from zero to nine, while the eight squares below each contained two numbers separated by a diagonal line.

Maya frowned. "It looks like a board game."

Napier's Bones

"It's an early calculator invented by a Scottish mathematician, inventor, and *scholar* named John Napier," Klart said as the rest of us gasped.

"Napier's Bones," I whispered.

"People called it that because they thought the wooden rods looked kind of like bones," Klart said.

Raven leaned forward. "How does it work?"

"It's really sort of amazing," Klart said, taking the rods out of the box. "Let's say you want to multiply seven times four. Just go down to the number seven on the left. Then go across to the rod with the number four at the top and—"

"Two eight," Maya chirped, reading the two numbers in the square Klart was pointing at. "The answer is twenty-eight."

"Right," Klart said. "Now let's try a harder one. How about six times four hundred and twenty-five?"

Klart took all the rods out of the box and handed Maya the three numbered four, two, and five. "Put them into the box next to each other so the numbers at the top form four hundred and twenty-five. Then go down to the six on the left and read the number on the top of the diagonal line on the first rod."

Maya put the three rods into the box and slid her finger down to the six. "The number on top of the first square is two."

"Right," Klart said. "Now add the numbers diagonal from each other on the bottom of the first square and the top of the second."

Maya slid her finger to the right. "Four plus one equals five."

Klart nodded. "Do it again with the next two rods."

"Two plus three equals five."

"And finally, the last number on the bottom of the final square."

"Zero," Maya said.

"There's your answer. Six times four hundred and twenty-five is two thousand, five hundred and fifty."

Maya laughed. "That's easy."

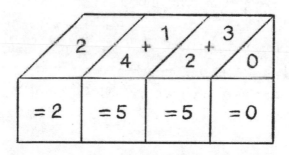

Klart nodded. "You can also do division, fractions, square roots, and more. Now all we have to do is use Napier's Bones to solve the problem on the board."

"But won't you just get the same answer?" I asked.

"Yes, but this time we'll be solving the problem with the 'bones of a scholar long dead' instead of 'inside our head.'" Klart looked at Raven. "Do you want to help?"

Raven hesitated, but Klart waved her over as he placed the rods back into the box. "Come on, I've never used Napier's Bones before and I'm pretty sure we'll need to convert the fractions to decimals to solve this math problem with it. With two of us watching, we'll be less likely to make any mistakes."

Carefully checking the equations Raven had written, the two of them placed the correct rods into the box, saying the answers to each step out loud as they ran their fingers down the numbers on the left and across the squares to the right until they reached the final calculation.

"You do it," Klart said, sliding the box to Raven.

She shook her head, trying to push it back. "You're the math genius."

"But you're the one who solved the problem in the first place."

"Fine," Raven said. "But if I kill us all, I'm not taking the blame."

I lifted my hat to wipe the sweat from my forehead. "Could we be just a tiny bit more positive?"

Raven took a deep breath, touched the final number,

and said out loud, "The answer is point zero five, which expressed as a fraction is . . . *one-twentieth*."

For a second, nothing happened. Then the ceiling began lowering slowly down.

"I messed up again!" Raven shrieked.

"No!" Maya said, pointing to the mine tracks. "The grate's open. You solved it!"

"Let's go," I said, pushing Raven and Klart toward the opening.

"What about the last question?" Klart asked.

"Who cares?" I said, running toward the opening. "We solved the puzzle."

He hesitated for a second before following me toward the carts, but Raven pulled away, running to the last wall.

"You're nearly there, don't lose your way," she shouted, reading the problem quickly from the last whiteboard before it was destroyed. *"For each wrong choice, a price you'll pay."*

The ceiling was so low, I had to bend completely over, and Klart was on his hands and knees.

"Forget it!" I shouted. "There's no time."

She ignored me, reading faster. *"If the path you wish to lead, choose your course with wire and bead.* What does that mean?"

"No idea!" I screamed as the whiteboard shattered. "Come on."

Maya waved her hands. "The carts are starting to roll."

"Hold them until I get there," Raven called. Dropping to her hands and knees, she scrambled toward the opening while I helped Maya and Jack kept the first cart from moving.

"Hurry!" Klart yelled, pulling back the second projector cart. "These are heavier than they look."

The tracks were tilting farther and farther down. Soon we wouldn't be able to keep the carts from rolling into the darkness.

Raven was almost free of the room, just about to squeeze through the opening, when Klart reached out to take her hand. Instead of grabbing it, she spun around and crawled back into the room.

"What are you doing?" I screamed as my shoes began to slide on the loose gravel next to the tracks.

Raven didn't answer. Back at the center of the room, she dug through the math supplies as if she'd suddenly remembered life was a geometry test and she was in desperate need of a ruler.

"She's not going to make it," Maya said.

"Hang on as long as you can, but don't let the carts go down without you," I yelled, diving back into the room and squirming after Raven.

"Got it!" Raven cried, her face lighting up. Clutching something in her hand, she crawled toward me, the ceiling still lowering and forcing us to lie even flatter. I thought we were both going to be crushed, but just as my hand closed around hers, someone grabbed me by the legs and pulled me and Raven toward the tracks.

Raven yanked her feet out of the room just before the

ceiling slammed shut. I turned around to find Jack looking sweaty and pale.

"Get on the back one," Raven yelled, pushing Jack toward the second cart. She raced to the front projector cart and jumped on, then reached back to grab me.

"Take this," she said, pushing the item she'd gone back for into my hands. As the cart rolled forward, Raven hoisted Maya up and threw her back to Klart, who caught her with a surprised gasp.

"What did you do that for?" I shouted, looking back to make sure Maya was okay.

Raven grabbed the item out of my hands. "If I understand the last problem, we're going to need a lot of maneuvering room."

"What is that thing?" I called.

At that moment, the cart seemed to drop out from under us and my stomach shot up like an elevator racing to the top of a really tall building.

Raven's voice echoed next to me as we plummeted into the darkness. "An ab-a-cussssssss!"

CHAPTER 16

The Cart Ride

There are two kinds of kids in this world: the
kind who look at a projector cart and think,
"I bet I can ride that down the stairs," and the
kind who don't have to ask you to sign their cast
after they discover just how wrong they were.

Clinging to the edge of the projector cart—hands
clenched and feet braced on the bottom shelf—was like
riding the world's bumpiest roller coaster with no safety
bars, seat belts, or even seats. Overhead, the ceiling changed
from brick to rock supported by thick wooden beams. Once
or twice we had to duck to avoid dripping stalactites that
looked like something straight out of a Minecraft world.

Grinning wildly, Raven held up a rectangular wooden
frame strung with rows of large circular beads. I knew an
abacus was a kind of calculator even older than Napier's
Bones, but I'd never used one before.

"Why would you risk your life for that?" I shouted, my
teeth rattling as the projector cart bounced over an especially

rough section of track like a kid catapulted by the wavy slide at the park.

"This is what the last problem was talking about," she said. *"If the path you wish to lead, choose your course with wire and bead."*

"But why bother?" I asked, pressing my hat low on my head to keep it from blowing off. "We already got out of the math room."

"Look," she called, pointing to a math problem painted on the side of the wall as we zipped past. Hooking one arm through the handle of the cart, Raven held the abacus flat in front of her and started moving the beads. "I have to use this to solve the problem."

I leaned closer to get a better look. "How does it work?"

"Each of the beads are counters," she said, trying to hold the frame steady as we rattled and jerked. "The wires connected to the top and bottom are called rods, and the wooden bar going across them is called the beam. The four beads below the beam are ones and the two beads above it are fives. To add a number, you slide one bead toward the beam."

I thought I understood. "So, if you slid three beads up from the bottom, that would be three. And if you moved one down from the top, it would be eight?"

"Right." Our cart jounced over a bump in the tracks, and she quickly pressed her hand to the beads to keep them from moving. "The first column of beads on the right are ones. The second column is tens. The third is hundreds and on up all the way to the left."

It looked pretty cool, but I didn't understand the point of continuing to solve math problems or why we had to do it with an abacus until Klart shouted, "Watch where you're going!"

I looked up to see the rails split into a Y only a few dozen yards ahead. Each track disappeared into a separate tunnel with a different pattern of circles arranged in rows above it.

"I think we have to compare the beads on the abacus to the circles above the tunnel to figure out which way to go!" Raven shouted, her voice nearly drowned out by the rattling of the carts.

Holding the abacus up to the light of the projector behind us, she looked from the beads to the patterns and shouted, "Go left!"

"How?" I called as we passed a large metal lever set into the ground beside the tracks.

"By pushing that," Raven said, looking back over her shoulder at the lever as our cart passed it.

Behind us, Klart lunged for the lever, but his fingers slipped off the handle.

My pulse soared like a soda rocket from a soccer-field launchpad as we reached the Y and took a right turn so sharp that I nearly fell off.

"What happens if we go the wrong way?" I asked, barely able to hear my own voice as the wind whipped by us.

"I don't know," Raven yelled back, her words echoing off the walls. "But I don't like the looks of that."

Ahead, the bouncing green light of our projector revealed a pitch-black ceiling that seemed to move in dark waves. At our approach, hundreds of glowing red eyes opened.

"Is that—?" I started.

All around us, leathery black wings spread as dark shapes launched themselves from the walls and ceiling, surrounding us in a flying wave of horror.

"Bats!" Maya screamed, followed by a high-pitched squeal from behind us that I was pretty sure was Jack.

The bats responded with ear-piercing screeches of their own, spreading their jaws to reveal tiny sets of fangs.

"Do something," Raven yelled, covering her head as the bats dive-bombed us, their sharp talons digging at our heads and backs.

Holding onto my hat with one hand, I lifted the clunky

old projector from the cart and shined its bright beam into eyes of the attacking creatures.

"Watch where you're pointing that!" Raven called as we rattled out of the bat cave and rejoined the main track. "I can't see."

Another math problem blurred past to our left. I turned the beam in that direction, but it was too late.

Raven shook her head. "I missed it."

"Twenty-seven times eight," Klart yelled.

Slamming the projector back onto the cart, I spotted the next lever as Raven moved the beads.

"Right," she said.

I bent my knees, reaching for the lever, but she pulled me back. "You don't need to push that one, the tracks are already turned in the right direction."

As we sped by the opening, I caught a glimpse of boulders bouncing down onto the other track.

"Nice save!" Klart called.

"Another right," Raven said as reached the third set of tunnels.

I slapped the lever perfectly, shifting the tracks ahead of us to stay on the correct course.

"What made you decide to go back and check the last problem?" I asked as we sped around a curve so sharp we had to lean into it to keep from tipping over.

Raven laughed, her bright red hair flying as we flew over a bump so steep the cart's wheels temporarily left the track.

"It was because of you," she said, tapping the center of my forehead with the tip of one finger. "You're pretty smart."

We passed another math problem, and she moved the beads, calling out the direction as I pushed the lever.

"I don't understand," I said, almost starting to enjoy myself. "I told you to forget the last problem and get on the cart."

"That's true. But you also said that the easier a problem looked, the harder it probably was to solve, and the last problem was the easiest of all."

"Because we didn't need to solve it to get on the carts." I tapped her forehead back. "You're pretty smart yourself."

Raven smirked. "That was never in doubt."

"What if we'd done the problems in a different order?" I asked.

"I don't think it would have worked," Raven said. "That's why they numbered them. If we'd tried solving them out of order either nothing would have happened, or—"

"We would have been crushed."

"Right." She popped a piece of gum into her mouth as we zipped past the next math problem.

As she moved the beads on the abacus, she tried to blow a bubble, but the wind ripped the gum from the tip of her tongue.

"Left," she said, giggling as she watched her gum whirl out into the darkness.

Maybe we were getting overconfident, or maybe the fact that we hadn't faced anything dangerous since the bats made us forget how easily things could go wrong. Either way, we both made a tragic error.

Seeing that the track was set to turn us the right way, I raised my hands above my head like I was on a roller coaster. "Woo-hoo!"

Raven looked from her abacus back up to the patterns and gasped. "No, I was wrong! We need to turn right."

I lowered my arms, lunged for the bar . . . and missed.

Behind us, Klart looked up at the ceiling, not seeing what had happened. Maya spotted the problem, but her arms were too short to reach the lever.

"Gray!" Raven screamed.

I spun around to see that the set of tracks we were about to turn onto ended abruptly—the ground under them had broken away, leaving twenty feet of empty space with nothing but a plunge to the jagged rocks below.

With no time to think, I turned and jumped back toward the second cart. Unsnapping my elastic sticky hand, I pulled it from my belt, flicked my wrist, and stretched out my arm. I was tumbling through the air—there was no way my plan should have worked. But once again, my trusty friend came through in a pinch, smacking the top of the lever and sticking firm.

Unfortunately, my leap carried me too far, and I flew up and over the second cart.

"We've got you!" Klart bellowed as three sets of hands wrapped around my legs and pulled me back to the cart.

The lever moved, but it was too late for Raven. Halfway

through the turn, her cart's wheels screeched as it spun around and flipped her over right in front of us.

"Jump!" I shouted, reaching out for her.

She leaped. Arms and legs jumbled around each other as I held Raven while Klart, Maya, and Jack held me.

"Is everybody okay?" Klart yelled.

"I think so," Raven said, her voice shaking as she clutched the edge of the cart to keep her balance. "But I lost the abacus. We won't know which way to turn."

"I don't think that matters anymore," Maya said. "Look."

Craning my neck to see around Raven's foot that was poking up in front of my face, I saw that the track had flattened out. A few hundred feet ahead, the dark tunnel ended in a circle of light. The cart slowed to a coast until its wobbly wheels finally bumped to a halt at the end of the track.

"We made it," Raven said, untangling herself and sliding off the cart.

We'd survived the rails, but where had we made it to?

Blinking as we walked from the dark tunnel into a brightly lit hallway, I looked around.

"It's like we're back at the school," Maya said.

She was right. From the floor to the ceiling, it looked exactly like the inside of Ordinary Elementary. Except for the five identical doors spaced a few feet apart from each other down one side. Above them, a sign read,

Choice, Not Chance, Determines Your Destiny
—Aristotle

CHAPTER 17
Choice, Not Chance

When one door closes, another one opens.
The question you have to ask yourself
is, Do I really want to find out what's
on the other side of that door?

Klart groaned. "Another puzzle?"

"I don't think so," Raven said, standing in front of a podium across from the door.

Crowding around her, we each looked down at a sheet of cream-colored paper. The message on it was written in the kind of swooping letters people sometimes used to address the envelopes of wedding announcements or invitations to fancy parties.

*Congratulations, you have reached
the end of your quest. It is now
time to receive your reward.*

Below that was a poem also printed in the same fancy letters.

Like Sisyphus's rolling stone,
Claim a path to call your own.
All may choose a single way,
Or apart they each must stay.
Enter when the way is clear,
Press ahead, the time is near.
Think carefully before you choose.
The prize is yours to win or lose.

Maya looked up from the paper. "What does that mean?"

"It means we won!" Klart said. He raised his fist in the air and whooped. "We did it. Come on, let's get our reward."

"Wait," I said as he stepped toward the door directly behind him. "The poem says we all have to go through the same door together, or we'll be forced to separate."

Klart grinned. "Sounds good to me. Which door should we open? One, two, three, four, or lucky number five?"

"They all look the same," Maya said.

Raven walked to the first door. "There's writing on the knob. It says *Wealth.*"

"Money, money, money," Klart said. He hurried to the second door and read the words printed on its knob. "This one says *Power.*"

"Really?" Raven's eyes lit up as she came to see.

"*Fame,*" Maya said, checking the third door.

Jack ran to check doors four and five and whispered to Maya.

"He says the last two are *Knowledge* and *Legos*."

Klart laughed. "It's like *The Wizard of Oz*. 'If I only had a brain!'"

"Which one should we pick?" Maya asked.

"Easy," Raven said. "Power."

"Money," Klart said at the same time.

He frowned. "What are you talking about? If you have money, you can buy your way into power."

Raven shook her head. "Not necessarily. But once you have power, making money is easy."

Maya looked at them both. "I don't care about either of those. I just want—"

"Fame," I whispered. They all turned to look at me. "Back in the computer lab, Jack said he wanted all the Legos, and Klart said he wanted money. Then, when Maya and I were talking after we finished climbing the card catalog, I said I only hunted for treasure to know what it was and how it got there."

"Knowledge." Maya tilted her head. "But I said I wanted to be famous."

I turned to Raven. "Up in the math room, you said that the reason you answered the math question yourself was to prove you were powerful enough to lead the team. Whoever set this up knows exactly what each of us wants. They've been spying on us."

"Yeah, but they're giving us our dreams," Klart said. "Just like they promised at the start of the hunt. Who cares how they know? I just want to claim my moolah."

"Wait," I said as he started toward the first door. "This feels like a trap."

He turned slowly around. "What are you talking about?"

I looked from the message on the podium to the five doors. "Up in the math room, we all promised to get the treasure together and split it evenly. Now, we find a note that says we can all claim the treasure together just like we promised. Only the rewards listed on each of the doors are specifically designed to break us apart."

Raven sighed. "What does it matter? If we all go through the same door or each choose a different one, we're still splitting the treasure. The poem says so itself. *All may choose a single way, or apart they each must stay.* If we split up, we can have it all. Money, power, fame, knowledge and . . . Legos."

Jack nodded.

I pulled off my hat and shook my head. "That doesn't feel right."

"Are you serious?" Klart asked. "It feels exactly right. Don't you remember the message that started all this? *A treasure greater than any you can imagine.* This is it."

"I remember," I said. "But why put us through all of those tests only to make us choose separate paths? Why not let us finish together and then give us whatever we want? Let's take a few minutes to study the message again—figure things out."

Klart shook his head, backing toward the first door. "I don't need to figure anything out. I made it here, and I know what I want: enough hundred-dollar bills to fill a swimming pool. The rest of you can either come with me or go your own ways."

"Just stop for a minute and step away from the doors," I said. "Why rush in? We all solved the other tests together. We can solve this too."

"Only, what if we didn't?" Raven asked. "There was another part of the message. *Complete it first and the grail is yours.*"

Maya and Jack looked at me. "Didn't we already complete the quest?"

"Maybe." Raven edged toward the second door. "But look at the sign. *Choice, not chance, determines your destiny.* What if the hunt isn't over? What if the last test is choosing a door—*first?*"

Klart moved a step closer to his door.

"Both of you stop," I said. "Don't you remember what we talked about? How wanting the wrong kinds of things made us make bad choices? This is exactly what you said you didn't want to do anymore. If we all just trust each other, we can make sure we're doing the right thing."

"I trust *you*, Gray," Raven said, narrowing her eyes as she glanced to where Klart was nearly in reach of the knob of the first door. "If we all pick a door together, we all finish at the same time, and we all win. But if one of us—"

Klart lunged at the first door as Raven did the same with the second.

"Stop!" I shouted. "We all agreed to—"

But it was too late. Each of them pulled open their

doors at the same time and a thick gray mist rolled out from the openings. They both looked at each other, then dove inside. As the doors swung shut behind them, the knobs fell off with a pair of matching *klunks*.

"No," I said, gritting my teeth. "You promised."

Maya came over and squeezed my hand. "It's okay. They both ended up getting what they wanted."

"Did they?" I wasn't so sure. For some reason I kept thinking about those game shows where contestants picked a random door hoping to win a trip and ended up getting a rusty bucket.

"Let's go back and reread the poem," I said. "Maybe we missed something."

Jack sighed and whispered to Maya.

She bit her lower lip.

"What's wrong?" I asked.

"It's just . . . It's been a really long day. We haven't had dinner yet, and we still have school tomorrow. If we don't get home soon—"

"I get it," I said. "Your parents will worry. It's okay if you want to go."

"We could all go through the same door together," she said. "What do you think? Fame, knowledge, or Legos?"

I dropped my head. "I don't want to pick. Honestly, I'm not even sure they're real. This feels like what I was talking about back in the math room. The treasure is right out in the open. It's too easy."

Jack whispered to Maya, and she nodded. "Maybe that's

because you're thinking about this as a trap instead of a reward."

"Maybe." I pushed up my hat and ran my fingers through my hair. "It's getting late, and you've both been through a lot. We should probably finish this before your parents start worrying."

Maya started to say something then shook her head. "Jack, which one do you want?"

Jack pointed to the fifth door—Legos.

"I guess that leaves you with fame," I said to Maya. "Good luck. I hope it works out for you both."

"Thanks," Maya said, giving me a quick hug. "And we hope you get your knowledge." She walked Jack to his door, waiting until he opened it and stepped into the mist before turning to open the *Fame* door.

"Wait," I called, running toward her as the dark mist curled out.

But it was too late. Maya gave me a small wave before I could get there and stepped through.

"Great job," I muttered to myself, feeling like a total failure as Maya's door swung shut and the knob dropped to the floor. Why couldn't I keep a group together? Why wasn't I a better leader? A better friend?

A treasure hunter didn't just charge into the treasure room. A treasure hunter researched all available information, considered every option, and made a careful plan to give themselves the optimal chance of success.

Why hadn't I managed to help my team see that?

I trudged back to the podium and studied the poem again. I was sure I was missing something. I just didn't know what.

"All may choose a single way." Clearly we'd messed that up. "Or apart they each must stay." Even the Oracle couldn't have predicted that any better.

"Think carefully before you choose." *Right.* We'd barely finished reading the poem through once before everyone started going for the doors. "The prize is yours to win or lose." That was interesting. If the doors really opened to what they promised, how could you lose the prize?

I knew there had to be something else here. Something important. I studied the first two lines carefully. "Like Sisyphus's rolling stone, claim a path to call your own."

That was an odd reference. Sisyphus was a man from Greek mythology who Zeus punished by making him push a rock up a hill for eternity. He definitely hadn't chosen his own path or received any kind of reward. Why use him use him as an example? Especially in the first line of the poem?

That left the last two lines: "Enter when the way is clear, press ahead, the time is near."

I rubbed my forehead, remembering what I'd just seen. The minute each of the other kids had pulled open their door, the entryway had filled with a thick mist.

"The way *wasn't* clear," I whispered, realizing I might have just let my friends make a huge mistake.

"Enter when the way is clear," I repeated. It was too easy. They'd all gone straight for the treasure and somehow they'd each set off a trap. But what could they have done differently?

"Press ahead, the time is near." Looking back up at the first line, I realized what I should have seen right away. Sisyphus didn't pull a rock up a hill. He *pushed* it.

"The words on the knobs didn't mean anything," I growled, balling my fists. "That was just a decoy to force us to split up."

It wasn't about *which* door we chose or who opened theirs first. It was about *how* they were opened. Klart, Raven, Jack, and Maya all pulled, setting off the gray mist when they should have pressed forward.

"Hang on, wherever you are!" I shouted, running to the final door. "I'm coming."

I grabbed the knob, turned it, and pushed. Instead of thick gray mist, I looked into a long, narrow hallway just in time to spot a hooded figure disappearing around a corner.

"Wait," I called, hurrying after them. "What did you do with my friends?"

Ducking its head, the figure moved faster, disappearing around corners as I hurried to catch up until we were both running down a series of narrow, twisting corridors lit only by flickering torches. As I raced down them, the hallways seemed to double back on themselves like a coiled snake.

"Stop!" I shouted. "I have questions."

Holding out my hands to keep from banging into the walls of the dimly lit passage, I turned a corner and ran straight into the biggest spiderweb I'd ever seen.

I backed away, ripping the sticky webs from my face and hands. I hadn't passed any intersections or doors where the robed stranger could have turned, but clearly they hadn't come here. I must have missed something.

Deep in the dark hallway metal gleamed in the sputtering light. I peered closer, trying to make out the source of the shine and spotted something moving. The web I'd walked into was gently swaying with the weight of dozens of enormous—

"*Spiders*," I muttered trying to hide the way my legs trembled. "Why does it have to be spiders?"

Hadn't I already proved myself by coming this far? I looked at the torch on the wall and thought about using it to burn away the web. But that wasn't fair to the spiders, even if they were nearly the size of my hand. Just because I was scared of them didn't give me the right to destroy their home.

Studying the web, I thought I saw another way. The main web was made up of a series of tightly packed circles spiraling slowly outward to where the biggest circle attached to an outer border that filled the hall from floor to ceiling.

There was no way I could get through the

145

center of the web without destroying it and likely being attacked by the enraged arachnids. But by shifting a couple of the frame's anchor points, I might be able to move the web up just enough to let me crawl under one corner.

"Okay, kids," I said, trying to keep my voice from trembling. "I don't want to bother you, and you don't want to bother me. Let's do just enough rearranging to get what we both need without any of us getting injured."

Using a pair of curved-jaw pliers from my archaeology kit, I clipped the bottom right thread. For a moment the web trembled and the spiders began to move in my direction. But when I reattached it to the wall about eighteen inches up, they went back to what they were doing.

One by one, I moved each of the anchor strings until I had formed a big enough space to slide through.

"Thanks, gang. It was great working with you," I said as I grabbed my pack and slid through the opening.

On the other side, I found what I had seen earlier: a black and gold metal door covered with hieroglyphics. Beside it was an ancient gong at least twice as tall as I was. The metal was so tarnished that I could barely make out the familiar protractor-shaped symbol with its seven stars and all-seeing eye.

I grabbed the mallet hanging from the frame of the gong, lifted it above my head, and swung.

As the metal circle rang with a deep echoing *gong-ong-ong-ong*, the door slid open and a robed figure who might or might not have been the same one I'd been following held out a hand. "Welcome."

Gripping my hand, the figure pulled me through the door into a circular room filled with chairs, couches, and what looked like a snack bar. They reached up to sweep back the hood of their robe, revealing a face I'd never expected to see in person.

I gasped. "Principal Redbeard?"

CHAPTER 18
The Illuminerdy

If someone offers to make your every wish come true, there's almost always a catch.

"Well, it's really more gray than red these days," Principal Redbeard said, tugging at the whiskers that covered the lower half of his face before disappearing down into the front of his robe. "But I guess that happens when you get to be my age."

"Congratulations!" said another robed figure walking toward me. He was a dark-haired boy about my age with brown skin and an amused grin. "I can't believe how fast you figured out the card catalog. I fell back into that disgusting water like five times before I realized there had to be a pattern. My name's Carter, by the way."

"I'm Rory," said a tall white girl with blonde hair who looked like she was at least two or three years older. Her freckled nose wrinkled as she laughed. "I can't believe your librarian remembered me. I thought I was being so sneaky." She held up her hand to give me a high-five and I was so surprised that I slapped her palm without thinking about it.

An Asian girl with dark hair cut short on one side and

long on the other held up a stopwatch. "I'm Ann and that's Michael. You beat his time by almost forty-five minutes."

"People call me Fire Plug," said a small, pale, red-haired kid who was missing his top two teeth. "The only reason you beat my time is because you cheated. He never would have made it through the math room if those other kids hadn't helped him."

"Wait, I think I recognize you," I said. "Aren't you the kid who stole the medal from me?"

The red-haired boy nodded. "That kid with you was fast, I've never had anyone come that close to catching me."

"Nice clown costume."

"It wasn't a costume," the boy said. "I'm a certified clown, master juggler, and expert acrobat. I perform all over the world."

I was pretty sure he was joking, but he didn't smile as he said it.

Principal Redbeard shook his head and tugged at his beard. "Mr. Foxx did not cheat, Michael. The only rule to the contest is that there are no rules to the contest. That's what makes it such a valuable measure of future success. Vanessa completely skipped the projector carts and walked down the rails like a balance beam. Steve used a grappling hook on the card catalog, and Ann skipped the math room entirely by peeling back the front of the whiteboards to re-program the circuits."

The Asian girl pumped a fist in the air. "Only one to get through the entire room in less than three minutes."

TV screens set high on the walls showed pictures of me and my friends at different parts along our hunt and white text with things like time, accuracy, and projected success rate. "What's going on?"

"It's totally okay to be confused," said a girl with bronze skin, blue eyes, and glasses. "Sometimes we get so excited to watch another person taking the test that we forget what it's like to be on the other side." She held out one hand. "I'm Dr. Samantha Ferriera."

I blinked. "Doctor?"

"Don't get her started," Fire Plug said. "She loves to brag about how she's the youngest surgeon ever."

Samantha rolled her eyes. "I'm still finishing my residency. But I do hope to specialize in organ transplants in another few years. I've got some ideas that could easily add another ten years to the average lifespan."

"Stop!" I shouted, holding up my hands. "I don't know

who any of you are or what you're doing here, and I don't care. All that matters is where Maya, Jack, Raven, and Klart are. What did you do to them?"

All around the room, the kids who had been laughing and joking turned to stare at me.

"Why does it matter?" Rory asked. "They lost."

"Your friends are fine," Principal Redbeard said. "I promise. Each of their passages led them safely out of the school. By now they're almost home." He pointed to the chairs and couches at the center of the room. "Please take a seat and I'll explain everything to you."

I opened my mouth to argue, but he held out one hand. "I promise they are okay. Let me answer your questions and I think you'll understand."

"If you're lying, I'll make sure every one of you regret it," I said.

"Sounds like we have a tough guy," Carter whispered, and the other kids all laughed.

"He doesn't seem very grateful to be here," Dr. Samantha said.

"Trust me," Ann said. "You're going to be amazed when you hear what Mr. Sullivan has to say." She pointed to a couch. "Sit down and prepare to have your life changed."

"Okay," I said. "But if this is another test and you're about to throw me into a pool of sharks or something, at least give me enough warning so I can hold my breath."

"I promise, no sharks," Principal Redbeard said with a grin. He and all the kids took their seats around me. "The test is really and truly over, and now it's time for you to claim your prize."

"What prize?" I asked, honestly curious.

"Great question," Principal Redbeard said. "What prize would you like?"

I felt almost as annoyed as the time the cafeteria ran out of corndogs just as I got to the front of the lunch line, so I had to eat a chicken patty that tasted like cardboard and gluey mac and cheese. "I thought you said the test was over."

"It is," Principal Redbeard said. "All that's left is deciding what you've won."

I looked around to see that all of the other kids were watching me with excited smiles. "Okay, fine," I said. "A treasure chest full of gold coins and jewels."

"Wish I'd asked for that," Michael said.

Principal Redbeard's smile disappeared. "Is that really what you want? It's not what you said out there." He put a hand to his chin. "Let's try this another way. What is the greatest treasure you can imagine?"

I thought for a moment. "A full kit of professional archaeology supplies."

Behind me, someone giggled, and Principal Redbeard silenced them with a stern look.

"A good choice. But anyone with a wallet full of credit cards can buy those things."

This was harder than I'd expected. I'd hunted lots of treasures but usually they were just whatever came up. It had always been more about the search than the reward for me. "Okay, money," I said, thinking of the things Klart had said before opening the first door. "Because you can buy whatever you want with it."

The kids around me muttered something I couldn't make out, but it didn't sound positive.

"People make—and lose—billions of dollars every day," Principal Redbeard said, looking like he was wondering if maybe he'd picked the wrong kid after all. "If you could have one thing, what would it be? I'll give you a hint. It's not power or Legos or fame."

Sweat ran down my back, and I suddenly got the feeling this was the real test. That everything else had only earned me the opportunity to answer this one question. What did people ask for in the movies when they rubbed a magical lamp? Cash? Big houses? Love? More wishes?

Suddenly I remembered the symbol on the back of the spelling bee medal. The symbol that had led me here in the first place. *Intelligence above all.*

I relaxed my fingers I hadn't even realized that I'd curled into fists. "Intelligence."

"Very good," Principal Redbeard said as the kids around me clapped. "Intelligence is the greatest treasure because it can never be bought, sold, borrowed, or stolen. And yet it has affected more lives than all the other powers on Earth combined."

"Okay, sure," I said. "But you can't actually give me in-telligence."

"Nobody needs to," Dr. Samantha said. "We all proved we have it by getting here."

"True," Principal Redbeard agreed. "We only accept the very brightest children in the world. What we *can* do is let you use it in ways that you can't imagine."

I was starting to get interested. "Like what?"

He folded his hands together. "You consider yourself an amateur archaeologist."

"I mean, I'm not *totally* amateur," I said bristling at the man's tone. "I've actually got—"

He waved his hand, cutting me off. "How many of the classes you take every day are on archaeology?"

"None," I said. "They don't offer any here."

He nodded. "How would like to train at the Smithsonian in Washington, DC?"

I felt my mouth open, but no words came out.

"What about apprenticing with a team of paleontologists from the American Museum of Natural History?"

This had to be a joke. I waited for someone to laugh, but nobody did.

"You can do that?"

"That and so much more," he said.

Suddenly my whole body began to itch, and I wondered if I was breaking out in hives. I scratched the back of my neck. "You're talking about, like, years from now after I graduate from college and stuff, right?"

"How old do we look to you?" Fire Plug asked, grinning to show his missing teeth.

Principal Redbeard shook his head. "If you agree to join us, you may begin as soon as next week."

I felt myself starting to hyperventilate, and my knees began to wobble. I'd had dreams like this before, but never anything that felt this real.

"How could one person possibly offer all of that?"

"One person by themselves couldn't," he said, gesturing toward the kids sitting around me. "But thousands of the most brilliant minds banded together could—and do."

He reached into his pocket and pulled out a silver ring. "Long before any of us here were born, my family amassed more riches than they would be able to spend in a thousand lifetimes. Realizing their money was the result of their incredible brain power, and understanding the responsibility that came with it, they invited the smartest men and women in the world to join a group they called the Illuminerdy."

CHAPTER 19
A Big, Costly Decision

Being a kid means making decisions.
Which shoes should I wear? Should I eat
cereal or frozen waffles? Ride my bike or
take the bus? Should I join an incredibly
powerful super-secret organization or not?
Some decisions are bigger than others.

I tilted my head. "The Illumi-what?"

"*The Illuminerdy*," he repeated. "People who had been teased as children. Called names like nerds and geeks."

"Bookworms," Rory said.

"Dweebs, brainiacs, weirdos, and a lot worse," Ann added.

"But those same people later became the movers and shakers of the world," Principal Redbeard said. "Artists, authors, scientists, doctors, financiers, inventors, politicians."

I looked back at the kids around me.

"Mankind's greatest hope has always been that these brilliant minds could mold the world into something better—led by those whose intelligence was far above their peers. The problem is that once people become successful, they are usually too old and set in their ways to do anything that might challenge their current status. Which is why we turned to—"

"Kids!" I blurted. "That's why your family donated to Ordinary Elementary. You decided to build schools, and libraries, and—"

Principal Redbeard puckered his lips like he'd just tasted a sour gummy worm. "Not exactly."

"Schools stink," Carter muttered.

Principal Redbeard shook his head. "Once, long ago, public schools might have been the best place to shape great young minds like yours. But if that ever was the case, it isn't now. Do you really think you'd learn more listening to some teacher drone on about boring statistics and memorizing how to spell geography than you would by joining archaeological digs, preserving artifacts, and exploring ancient civilizations?"

I shook my head. "No. But I mean, who would let someone my age do that?"

"We would!" Rory shouted.

Principal Redbeard nodded. "The Illuminerdy locates the most intelligent children in the world through tests like you just took, pulls them out of stifling school, and offers them opportunities most kids can only dream about. My great-great-great grandfather built this school as the first recruiting center. He named it Ordinary Elementary precisely because it was designed to pull the few extraordinary children out from their very ordinary peers."

"If your group is so big and powerful, why haven't I heard of the Illuminerdy before?"

"An excellent question," Principal Redbeard said. "We prefer to work in secret. Some people would object to the fact that we provide our resources only to the smartest children—those with the greatest chance to make a difference."

I frowned. "When you say 'make a difference,' are you talking about just making the world better or making it into what *you* think it should be?"

For a brief second, Principal Redbeard's eyes darkened. Then his smile returned. "That is up to you, my boy. As part of our group, you'll help decide how to make the world better. So what do you say?" He held up his ring. "Do you want to leave your humdrum elementary school behind and challenge that great brain of yours with some *real* learning?"

The kids behind me let out a cheer, hooting and hollering.

I tried to get it all straight in my head. "You're saying that if I join your group, I can study whatever I want wherever I want. And the Illuminerdy will pay for it all?"

"Not *everything*," Rory said. "I'm still trying to get my own private jet."

Principal Redbeard laughed. "Even *we* have to manage our finances. But for the most part, yes. You decide what you need to make the biggest difference, and we help you get there. Exploring the past to make a better future?

Translating ancient languages? Discovering forgotten species? Uncovering the secrets of lost civilizations? Just say the word."

It all sounded amazing. I hadn't felt this excited since I bought my first set of archaeology brushes. "Okay," I said. "I'll do it. But I need to go get my friends so they can join too."

"You can't," Carter said. "They failed the test."

"No, they're actually the ones who solved most of it. They just went through the doors wrong before we figured out the last message."

"They *failed* the test," Carter repeated more firmly. "They didn't solve the last puzzle."

I shook my head. "You're saying my friends can't join your group because they pulled a door instead of pushing?"

"I'm saying they weren't up to our standards," Principal Redbeard said as calmly as if he were explaining why preschoolers took naps and fifth graders didn't. "It's not an insult. We test thousands of applicants a year. Less than one percent pass."

"But I wouldn't have passed either if it wasn't for them. Klart figured out most of the math problems. Raven went back for the abacus. Maya and Jack realized we needed to turn the bell. It was a team effort."

Principal Redbeard folded his arms as he walked slowly around the room. "Teams are useful for building barns and digging wells. But when it comes to the things that really matter, they hold you back. Group projects almost never work out because there is one leader and a bunch of lazy drones. The Illuminerdy isn't in the business of recruiting drones. We're looking for leaders."

"But how do you know that you aren't missing lots of other kids who might be just as successful, or even more, if they had access to the same resources? My friends are at least as smart as me, if not smarter. And what about the kids who never get a chance to take your test because they don't think the same way you—"

He held up one hand. "I understand your concerns, and we have considered the possibility. But the truth is, any one of my students could think circles around a hundred non-exceptional children. And that is why we put our money where it can do the most good."

"With people like us," Ann said.

I couldn't believe what I was hearing, and that everyone in the room was going along with it.

"You're saying that everything you put my friends through was for nothing?" I waved my hands. "The alligators, the collapsing math room, the mine carts. They could have died."

"Simple theatrics, combined with convincing special effects. Do you think we would have put a brain as valuable as yours in real danger?"

I shook my head, not sure what I believed anymore.

Principal Redbeard coughed into his fist. "You tried to convince your so-called friends to wait before going through the doors. Why didn't they?"

"Because you tricked them," I said.

"Nobody tricked anyone," Rory said. "They just didn't listen to you."

Principal Redbeard pointed his remote to one of the screens and replayed a video of me trying to convince Klart and Raven to wait. "Your friends ignored your warning because they were greedy. Because money and power were more important to them than making a good decision. They did exactly what ordinary people in this world do every day."

He froze the screen and turned to point at me, holding out the Illuminerdy ring. "Do you want to spend the rest of your life talking to greedy, selfish, unintelligent people who will never listen to what you have to say? Or do you want to join people who, like you, value intelligence above all?"

I licked my lips, my hands sweating like a popsicle on a windowsill.

"Think carefully," he said. "Because we only ask once. And we don't take *No* well."

I reached down to touch the elastic sticky hand on my belt. "Are you threatening me?"

Carter rubbed a hand across his mouth. "It's not just a threat," he whispered.

"It's called the Curse of the Illuminerdy." Principal Redbeard chuckled deep in his throat, the sound as threatening as a vicious guard dog about to attack. "We don't have to use it often because we don't make our offers lightly. Nearly everyone we invite to join us says yes. If you do not—"

"What?" I asked, trying not to show that I felt as scared as a kid trying to ride a bike without training wheels for the first time. "Are you going to throw me back into the pool with the alligators?"

He shook his head. "The Curse of the Illuminerdy makes getting eaten by alligators feel like a vacation."

Sweat beaded on my forehead. Nobody makes it as a treasure hunter without facing their share of bullies, but Principal Redbeard felt more dangerous than the rest of them combined. His eyes didn't look like he was bluffing, and a part of me really wanted to accept his offer. But I'd promised to share the treasure if I found it.

Slowly I reached up, gripped the brim of my fedora, and tugged it low over my eyes. "I'd rather spend the rest of my life being completely ordinary with my real friends than spend one more minute with you and your egotistical Illuminerds. My answer is *no!*"

CHAPTER 20
Truths and Lies

Honesty is the best policy. Unless honesty
will destroy your life as completely as a two-
year-old standing next to a tower of blocks.
Then you have to consider your options.

The minute I set foot on the school playground the next morning, Maya, Jack, Raven, and Klart were on me like kittens on a cotton ball.

"So," Klart said, trying to bounce a basketball but not doing a very good job of it. "Time to confess."

"What are you talking about?" I squeaked. Hopefully the Illuminerdy's threat had been a bluff, but either way, I didn't see any point in telling my friends what I'd been offered—or why I'd turned it down.

Klart bounced the ball off his shoe and had to run to get it before it rolled in front of a school bus. "Which one of us got the treasure?"

"Oh, right," I said, taking a deep breath as my heart started to beat again. "Who did?"

"Not me," Maya said. "As soon as I stepped through the

door, the air was filled with this weird smoke, and I couldn't see anything. I wandered down this really long corridor, hoping I'd eventually end up in a treasure room or something. Instead, I fell through a hole into a drainage pipe that came out at a creek on the other side of the school. It totally ended up ruining my favorite pair of shoes. Although, they were probably already ruined when we fell into the pool."

I looked at Klart, trying to play it casual. "You and Raven went through your doors first. Did you find anything?"

"Totally won the jackpot," Klart said. "Don't I look super rich?" He rolled his eyes. "My experience was even worse than yours, Maya. I couldn't see where I was going either. I kept walking and walking until I seriously thought I must be in another county. Finally, I found a door. I opened it and turned on the light, thinking I was going to see a huge pile of cash. Instead, I found myself in Mr. Flickersnicker's office with his three-legged cat standing between me and the door."

"How did you get away?" I asked. I'd faced Slayer once, and I never wanted to do it again.

Klart started to bounce the ball before shaking his head and tucking it under his arm. "I didn't. I had to wait there until the janitor found me. Now I have to pick up trash all next week as a punishment."

"Stay out of the Forsaken Field," Maya warned.

"Where did he get that?" Klart asked, pointing at Jack,

who was eating a giant pineapple cotton candy on a stick. "The carnival isn't even open yet."

Jack just shrugged and smiled.

Maya snorted. "He bugged the lady setting up the machines until she gave him one to go away."

"What happened after he went through the Lego door?" I asked.

Klart raised an eyebrow. "If he got the Harry Potter castle set, I'm going to be crying all week."

"No Legos," Maya said, eyeing her twin's cotton candy. "But he doesn't seem too broken up about it."

I grinned. How could I possibly leave those two—even for something as cool as training at the Smithsonian? "He won't tell you what happened to him?"

"He told me," Maya said. "Unfortunately, his version of what happened involves a giant toad, juggling axes, meeting a group of clowns who asked him to join their circus, and finally getting them to drive him home in their tiny car."

"Maybe that really happened," Raven said. "I mean, we did see some pretty weird things down there."

"Don't ask him to prove it," Maya said.

Raven smirked down at Jack. "Why not?"

With a smile, he unzipped his hoody, opened one side, and turned to show her a flower pinned to the front of his shirt.

When Raven leaned in to get a closer look, he squeezed a plastic bulb in his other hand and squirted water out of the flower into her face.

"Uckkk," Raven squealed, blinking water out of her eyes. "You little pest."

"Told you," Maya said.

"Well." Klart looked from Raven to me. "That just leaves the two of you. Please tell me that after everything we went through, at least one of us got something good."

Raven glared at me. Even though I knew she couldn't possibly have any idea what happened, I still felt a volleyball of doom form in the pit of my stomach. "Gray somehow always manages to figure out the puzzles."

I stared out at the carnival tents, unwilling to look any of my friends in the eye. It wasn't just that I'd solved the puzzle—and turned down the opportunity of a lifetime. It was that I wasn't sure how to explain the Illuminerdy's offer without sounding as big-headed as they were. "Pretty much the same as the rest of you. I, um, went through the door into the hallway."

"With the gray mist," Klart said.

"Right, right." I nodded. "Super thick mist. Couldn't see a thing."

Maya grinned. "Where did you come out?"

"Oh, you know." I stalled, trying to think of something. I was a terrible liar—especially with all four of them staring at me. "It was, like, totally dark. And there were these, um, spiderwebs. And I had to push through them, which was super disgusting. When I got to the other side, I came out the back door of the cafeteria and walked straight into the side of a dumpster."

Klart cracked up. "Classic. Okay, Raven, your turn."

All I wanted was for Raven to say that she hadn't won anything either so we could put it all behind us. The more I thought about the Illuminerdy's offer, the more they disgusted me.

"Fine," Raven said, with an embarrassed grin. "I'll admit it. I won."

"What?" I stared at her, trying to figure out what she was up to. I'd seen her pull the door open and step into the mist, which meant she'd followed an empty corridor as well.

"Serious?" Klart asked. "So, what's the deal? Are you, like, powerful now?"

"Well." Raven lifted her chin and shook back her red hair. "I don't like to brag."

Maya glared. "Since when?"

"It was all pretty fantastic," Raven said, ignoring Maya's furious stare. "As soon as the door closed behind me, the mist disappeared, and I saw this woman wearing a power suit. Seriously, like seven-hundred-dollar shoes and a cashmere blazer that must have cost at least a couple thousand dollars."

"Woah," Klart said, leaning so far forward it looked like he was about to tip over. "What happened then?"

Raven glanced around the playground as though making sure no one else was listening. "Well, we got into this private helicopter and flew into the city where we landed on top of a skyscraper. It turns out this woman is super connected to, like, all the most powerful people. And we went down into this enormous suite where they were having a party. And guess who I met?"

Even though I knew she was lying, I wasn't sure I wanted to call her out in front of everyone.

"Who?" Klart asked.

Maya sniffed. "Probably somebody boring."

Raven examined her nails. "I guess, if you consider Taylor Swift boring."

"What?" Klart shouted so loud that several of the kids playing clear over by the swing sets turned to look.

I glanced around, hoping none of the Illuminerdy's spies were watching. I didn't want them to think we were talking about them.

"Keep it down," Raven whispered, putting a hand to her mouth. "But Tay Tay and I ended up talking all night and now we're totally besties, and she said she might let me help her write a new song."

"Dude," Klart said. "So it really worked, and now you're powerful."

Raven shrugged. "Let's just say if I suddenly go missing this summer, you might want to go looking for me at a large building in Washington, DC, that goes by the initials W.H."

Jack threw the last of his cotton candy on the ground and whispered furiously to Maya. "It's not fair," she agreed.

"We promised that we'd split the treasure between all five of us, right, Gray?"

"Right." I felt like a total jerk for not telling them all the truth. But how could I explain that I'd been offered the prize, but I couldn't share it with my friends because the Illuminerdy didn't consider them smart enough to receive it? And besides, if the curse was real, even telling them about it might get them cursed as well.

Raven glared at me, before holding up her hands. "Power isn't like money or toys. You can't just break it into pieces. But I'll see what I can do."

"I'm not really into that kind of music," Klart said. "But if you ever run into someone like Pirateska Rebellion or the Interrupters, you have to introduce me."

"Come on," Maya said, pulling Jack by the arm, "Let's get out of here. I feel like I want to puke."

"Well, we all better get to class before the bell," I said, hurrying toward the school.

Raven edged up beside me and dropped her voice. "Is there something you want to tell me?"

"Nope," I said, almost running until we reached the school doors. "Except, you know, congratulations on Taylor Swift and the White House, and all that. You totally deserve it."

She clenched her jaw and glared at me. "This isn't over, Foxx."

CHAPTER 21
The Curse of the Illuminerdy

Some days you wake up, see the sun shining, hear the birds singing, remember you finished your homework the night before, and realize how great it is to be a kid. Other days you open your eyes, remember you've been cursed by the Illuminerdy, and wonder if it's too late to run away and join the circus.

I knew it was going to be a bad day the minute I stepped through the school entrance. Mrs. Zielinski, the school secretary, was usually the most cheerful person ever, but as I walked past her desk, she sized me up like a ham and cheese on rye that had sat in the back of the fridge so long it started growing mold.

"We have a problem, Mr. Too-Good-to-Go-to-School."

I glanced over my shoulder, thinking she must be talking to some schlub with an attendance problem. Turns out that I was the schlub.

"Do you know how many absences you are allowed in a quarter?" she asked, tapping one of her pens on the table.

I wondered if it was a trick question. "Um, three?"

"Five," she said, as though that explained everything. "Six if you have a signed slip from your doctor."

I nodded. "Well, thank you. That will be good to know if I ever come down with a bad case of the flu."

She shook her head like I'd let her down. "Do you know how many absences you have this quarter?"

This was an answer I knew. "One, because I had a rash on the back of my neck that my mom thought might be chicken pox. It turned out it was just the new laundry detergent."

I started to walk away, glad we'd had that little conversation, when she called me back. "Incorrect, you have nineteen."

I spun around. "What?"

She slapped down a stack of absence slips thicker than a thirty-dollar steak. "Take these home to get signed by your parents. And plan on staying after school until at least the end of January to make them up."

I thumbed through the slips, thinking it was some kind of joke, when a pizza delivery guy pushed the button at the front door and the secretary buzzed him in. "Can I help you?"

"Two large pizzas for a Graysen 'Ordinary' Foxx?"

171

"That's me," I said. "But I didn't order anything."

Mrs. Zielinski narrowed her eyes. "Students are not allowed to get food delivery at school."

"I know," I said, trying to fit the absence slips into my pants pocket.

"Says here these are from a Mr. PR," the pizza guy said. He shoved the pizzas into my arms and held out his hand for a tip. The only thing I had to give him was the absence slips. They didn't seem to impress him much and he headed back out to his car, muttering about cheapskates.

"What's that smell?" Jake "Toes" Campbell asked, walking toward me. "Please tell me it isn't my feet."

I read the top of the first pizza box. *Camembert cheese with anchovies and extra garlic.* "It's not your feet," I said.

He smiled. "Thank goodness. Anyway, I just wanted to thank you for signing up to sing a solo in the Halloween play this afternoon. We thought we were going to have to make it through without a musical number, so you offering to sing *Three Little Witches* is a lifesaver." He shoved a stack of sheet music into my arms. "See you at 2:00!"

"What?" I asked. "I didn't sign up for—" But he was already walking away, singing a song from the show I was now apparently in.

"What was that all about?" Maya asked, walking through the door behind me.

I shook my head. "I'm not positive, but I think somebody's trying to send me a message."

Jack glanced at the pizza boxes.

"Help yourself," I said.

If there was one person who would always be happy to eat pizza, no matter the kind, it was him.

He took one sniff of the boxes, wrinkled his nose, and disappeared faster than the first hotdog off the grill at a pool party.

After ditching the pizzas in the nearest trash can, I went to class and slid into my usual desk near the back. Ms. Devencourt, the substitute teacher, looked up from her phone and frowned. "Is everything okay, Graysen?"

I was surprised she remembered my name. "Yes, ma'am. Thank you for asking." I was hoping I could buy a few minutes to figure out how I was going to get out of this latest mess, but she waved me forward.

"Could you come up here for a minute?"

I trudged up the aisle, wondering if the day could get any worse. It turned out it could.

When I reached her desk, Ms. Devencourt typed my name on her computer keyboard with a concerned expression.

"Is there a problem?" I asked.

She dropped her voice and leaned toward me. "I'm afraid there is. It's about your grades. I just got a notification that you're failing every subject."

"What?" I moved around her desk to look at the computer screen. "That can't be right."

"I'm afraid it is," she said pursing her lips. "An automated email has been sent to your parents alerting them of the problem. But if you don't get your grades up, I'm afraid you'll need to retake these classes over the summer. You might even need to repeat fifth grade."

"That's impossible," I said. "I've never—"

All at once I realized what must be happening. "This is all part of the Curse of the Illuminerdy," I muttered.

She looked over. "What?"

"Nothing," I said.

Up on the wall, the intercom speaker buzzed. "Ms. Devencourt, is Graysen Foxx there?" Principal Luna asked.

"Yes, he is," the substitute teacher said, studying me like I was a criminal on the FBI's Most Wanted list.

"Could you send him to the office? Principal Luna would like to speak with him."

"On my way," I said, wondering how long I was going to be grounded. From the looks the other kids in my class gave me as I got my backpack and walked slowly to the door, they were wondering the same thing.

I stepped out of the classroom door just as Mrs. Hall, the librarian, came around it.

"Graysen," she said in a strange tone of voice. "I was just coming to find you."

"You were?" I asked. "Is it about the medal I showed you? Because—"

She shook her head. "It's about your overdue books. I don't know how I didn't notice it earlier. But there are quite a few of them, and I'm honestly surprised. It's not like you to keep so many books out so long past their due dates."

I gritted my teeth. "No. It's not like me at all. But I'll be sure to find them and bring them in right away."

"Thank you," she said. "Here's a list."

It was three pages filled with titles from top to bottom.

By the time I reached Principal Luna's office, I was ready to confess to whatever she accused me of, from stealing the school mascot to wrapping the school bus in toilet paper.

Taking a seat in front of her desk, I held out my wrists. "Lock me up in detention and throw away the key. At least no one will be able to accuse me of missing school."

She frowned. "What?"

"Isn't that why you called me here?" I asked. "What did I do? Steal the second-grade hamster? Spend the drama club fund?"

Principal Luna shook her head. "What's gotten into you?"

I pushed up my fedora. "Aren't I in trouble?"

"Not that I've heard about," she said. "I just wanted to let you know that the cafeteria workers told me about your terrible food allergies. From now on they will make sure that you are only served unsalted crackers and brown-skinned bananas."

I nodded. "That sounds very, um, healthy."

CHAPTER 22
Spilling the Beans

Secrets are like Reese's Pieces. Once your friends
discover you have them, it's only a matter
of time until they convince you to share.

Walking back from Principal Luna's office, wondering whether I'd rather eat unsalted crackers for lunch or go retrieve my anchovy and garlic pizza, I spotted Jack and Maya's teacher, Mr. Mackey. He was taping a blue ribbon for best-decorated classroom on the door where Mr. Sullivan's portrait used to be.

"Congratulations," I said. "But what happened to the painting?"

Mr. Mackey shrugged. "Someone from the district took it. Apparently it's a *significant historical artifact.*"

I was pretty sure it wasn't the district who had taken the painting, but I didn't tell him that.

"Would you like to come in and have some pizza with us?" Mr. Mackey asked. "Jack and Maya said we have you to thank for winning the contest."

I shook my head. "I don't have much of an appetite at the moment."

He nodded. "I hope it isn't a stomach bug."

Someone walked up from behind me and grabbed my arm. I spun around, thinking it was the Illuminerdy, but it was only Raven.

"Ready to tell me what really happened last night?" she asked.

"I don't know what you're—"

She shook her head. "I didn't believe you out on the playground this morning. Now, according to Lizzy and the second-grade spies, you've been accused of breaking more rules in one morning than I have in all the time I've been going to school here, and that's saying something."

"Lizzy doesn't work for you anymore," I said.

Raven smirked. "This one was on the house. The kids are worried about you, and I am too. Come on," she said, pulling me down the hallway. "I want to show you something."

I looked toward the clock, but she shook her head. "Don't pretend you have to get back to class. I know you still have the laminated hall pass, and your substitute teacher doesn't bother to take attendance half the time."

"Fine," I said, figuring twenty absences couldn't possibly be much worse than nineteen. "Lead the way."

Wondering if I was just adding to my problems, but no longer feeling quite so alone, I followed her down the hall and up the staircase Maya and I had climbed what felt like a lifetime before to the bell tower.

"Um, look, I know you have questions, and I should probably answer them. But now might not be the best time," I said, looking over my shoulder to make sure no one was watching. I wasn't sure exactly how the whole Illuminerdy curse thing worked, but I didn't want to take the chance of spreading it to her as well.

"Why not? The treasure hunt is over," Raven said. She studied me with an expression that made it clear she knew way more than she was letting on.

"What are you talking a—" I started to say when she slapped her palm against the side of the bell.

"Notice anything?"

I glanced toward it, started to say something, then looked again. The bell was the same shape and size as it had been, but the metal wasn't nearly as weathered. I didn't even need to look inside to know it wasn't the same one.

"I hear they replaced it the same time they took the painting," she said. "Almost like something happened to make them pull up stakes."

I took a deep breath. The girl was good. "Weird."

She snorted. "I'm guessing the projector carts are gone too. Which tells me the hunt is over."

"I d-don't know anything about that."

"Really?" She folded her arms. "Are you still going to pretend you didn't find the treasure?"

"I didn't," I said, hoping I could somehow bluff my

way through this. "You're the one who got to meet Selena Gomez."

"Taylor Swift." Raven shook her head. "I only said that because it was clear you were hiding something, and I didn't want the others to ask any questions. My door led to a garbage chute that dumped me out in the room at the bottom of the spiral staircase. Do you have any idea how embarrassing it is to have to call for help to get out of a grate in the floor of the girls' bathroom?"

"Sorry about that," I said. "But like I told you, I didn't win anything either. My door—"

She cut me off with a wave of her hand. "You're lying."

"What makes you think that?" I asked, trying to look innocent and failing worse than a kid trying to write a book report on a novel they've never opened.

Raven counted off the evidence on her fingers. "First, Klart, Maya, and Jack would have been shouting about it from the minute we saw them if any of them had found the treasure. Well, Jack would whisper, but still. Second, you claimed that you pushed your way through a bunch of spiderwebs, but everyone knows you hate spiders. You'd wait for days before pushing through a web of them—unless you knew there was a treasure behind it."

She had me there.

"Third, you said you ended up running into a dumpster outside the school. But the moment I realized I hadn't won, I staked out the school to see who came out when. Klart looked like he'd seen a ghost, but that was because of the janitor's cat. Jack did *not* arrive in a clown car. Maya climbed out of the creek a few minutes after her brother. You came out way after the rest of us, looking dazed and clearly having seen something none of the rest of us did. So, what gives?"

I wanted to tell her, but I couldn't risk it.

"I can't say," I muttered.

She tilted her head. "Why not? At first, I thought you were only cutting me and Klart out of our share of the treasure. But Maya and Jack swear you didn't share anything with them either. Was the treasure really so amazing that you wouldn't even share it with your two best friends?"

"There *is* no treasure!" I shouted, feeling like my head was going to explode. "I mean there was. But I don't have it. I turned it down."

Raven laughed. "Now I know you're lying. The day the Gray Fox turns down treasure is the day I let the entire school read my diaries."

"You keep diaries?" I asked. "Can I see them? As an archaeologist, of course."

She stuck out her tongue.

"I really can't tell you about it," I said. "I would if I could. But all the stuff about me breaking the rules is actually part of the curse I got for turning the treasure down. Just telling you about it could get you cursed too."

Raven sneered. "I eat curses for breakfast."

"I do too," Klart said, opening the door to the bell tower stairs he'd been hiding behind. "I mean, not *just* curses. I usually have eggs and toast too. And sometimes a bowl of Froot Loops."

"What are you doing here?" Raven growled.

Klart raised his eyebrows. "Hello? Spying? What does it look like?"

"We want to know too," Maya said, as she and Jack peeked over the railing.

"You two are supposed to be in class," I said.

"We're just having a pizza party, and Jack already ate six slices," Maya said.

Jack burped.

"Well, go back and have some more," I said. "You need to stay out of this."

"Sure," Maya said. "And miss hearing about treasure, espionage, and curses? That is *so* not happening. So where were we?"

"I'm not kidding," I said. "I'm not talking about some break-a-mirror-get-seven-years-of bad-luck kind of curse. I'm talking about people in powerful places who can destroy your education, your career, and your entire life."

"Men in Black," Klart blurted. "Please tell me that aliens set up this whole thing. Or that monsters are real, and we've been recruited to hunt them."

"Stop messing around," I said. "You're right. There was a treasure. But I really did turn it down. And because I did, they've promised to destroy my life."

"We don't like people threatening our friends," Maya said, her voice icy.

181

I groaned. "It's not a threat. It's already happening."

Klart leaned against the railing of the bell tower and scratched the back of his neck. "You might as well fess up, kid. We're not going to leave you alone until you tell us everything."

"We're not," Raven agreed. "You know me. I'll annoy you every day. Tap your phones, put listening devices in your classroom and GPS tracking on your bike."

I was pretty sure she didn't actually have that kind of technology. But I did know she wouldn't give up.

"Fine," I whispered, signaling for them all to crouch on the floor of the tower out of sight from anyone looking up. "But if you get cursed too, don't say I didn't warn you that your lives would be—"

"Destroyed," Raven. "We get it. Now, spill it all."

CHAPTER 23
A Daring Plan

There are times when the obstacle in front of
you is too big, the enemy too strong. When you
are outnumbered, overpowered, unprepared, and
out of options. Those are the times when it pays
to have friends who don't take no for an answer.

The minute I finished telling them what had happened,
Maya and Jack threw their arms around me.

"I can't believe you didn't tell us," Maya cried, squeezing
me so hard I could barely breathe.

"It's a way better story than the one about Taylor Swift,"
Klart said. "Especially since it's actually true. I can't believe
you turned down the chance to get out of this school and do
whatever you want."

"Is that all you got from that?" Raven asked.

"I mean, not *all*," Klart said. "But I have to say, it took
some serious guts to say no."

Jack whispered to Maya. "You turned it down for us?"
she asked.

I shrugged. "I turned it down because it was the only

fair thing to do. How could I have taken what they were offering and looked any of you in the eyes ever again? If it wasn't for the four of you, I never would have reached the treasure in the first place."

"But if we'd listened to you, we would have," Klart said. "We could have accepted the deal together."

Raven shook her head. "I'm not sure I could have."

"Whatever," Klart scoffed. "You're like the queen of selfishness when it comes to keeping treasure for yourself."

"Usually that's true," Raven said. "But that's when the treasure is something I can hang on my wall, or put in my trophy case, or use to make other people feel miserable because I have it and they don't. This . . ."

She shook her head. "We're talking about kids' education here—not some lucky yo-yo. If they really do have the kind of resources they say they do, and they're only sharing them with a tiny handful of students, it's like they're—"

"Deciding who has the chance to succeed and who doesn't," Maya said.

"Exactly. I mean, it's their money and they can do whatever they want with it. It just bugs me that there are kids who could make just as big of a difference in the world—maybe even more. But instead of giving those kids that chance, the Illuminerdy are only helping the kids who already have the advantage. It's like giving the person who's already winning a game a hundred extra dice rolls."

"Fine, it's terrible," Klart said. "But what does it matter? Gray turned down the treasure. The hunt is over."

"It would be," Raven said, "if they had taken no for an answer. But they didn't. Gray did what he felt was right, and now they're punishing him for it."

Jack whispered to Maya.

"He wants to know the plan for Operation Downfall."

I blinked. "Operation Downfall?"

Maya nodded. "That's the name he came up with for taking down the jerks that did this to you."

I stared at the four of them. "You want to—" I looked around and lowered my voice. "You want to attack the Illuminerdy?"

Klart started laughing. "Wait, that's what they call themselves? What kind of name is that?"

"You don't think we're going to let them get away with attacking one of our friends, do you?" Raven asked.

"I don't think you understand who you're going up against," I said. "They have politicians, business leaders, educators, tech gurus. In thirty minutes, they managed to sabotage pretty much every part of my school career. There's no way the five of us can defeat them."

Klart snorted. "I mean, it's not like the school network is particularly secure."

"Why do you think the Illuminerdy hit you so hard, so fast?" Raven asked.

"Because they don't like being told no," I said.

She nodded. "I mean, yes, that's part of it. But the real reason is that you not joining them threatens the one thing that gives them power."

"Money?" Maya asked.

"Followers," I said. "Connections."

"Computers," Klart guessed. "Technology. Enough personal data to destroy someone's life with a click of a mouse."

Raven shook her head. "Secrets." She turned to Klart. "What would happen to the Doodler if Principal Luna and the rest of the school knew about all the shady activities he's been involved in here?"

Klart puffed out a long slow breath. "Detention for life? Expulsion? Definitely losing his closet and the old art room he uses for his offices."

"Sure," I said. "But he's just a school bully."

"The Illuminerdy are just bullies too," Raven said. "The only way they keep their power is by operating in secret. That's why they're so paranoid. Once you expose a bully to the rest of the world, they're just another anxiety-ridden kid with questionable drawing talent and a juice-box problem."

"Okay, but these guys are like an unstoppable force of nature," I said. "Their members include politicians, scientists, bankers. And they've got billions of dollars. They could destroy us all before we even knew they were coming."

Maya wrinkled her forehead. "So that makes it okay for them to hurt innocent people?"

"Maybe not okay. But it makes them pretty much impossible to stop."

"Not in my book. It just means that they won't be expecting a handful of kids like us to make their organization crumble like stomping on a stale oatmeal cookie."

"Nice metaphor," I said. "But where would we even start?"

Raven thought for a minute. "They attacked us in our home. I say that we attack them in theirs."

I shook my head. "How do we know they even have a home?"

"Every villain has a lair," Klart said. "It's an unwritten rule."

"They're right," Maya said. "And this is where it all started, which means it's probably close by."

I looked at the five of them. "You really want to do this, understanding that we probably have zero chance of success?"

Klart held his thumb and first finger a fraction of an inch apart. "I give us at least a zero, zero, zero, zero, zero, point one percentage chance of success. And remember, I'm the math genius here."

Jack whispered to Maya. "We're in," she said.

Klart nodded. "Me too."

I shrugged. "I guess I've probably faced worse odds. Although I don't know when."

Raven grinned. "Then it's decided. Meet me in front of the junior high in fifteen minutes."

CHAPTER 24
Intruders

I love it when a plan comes together.
Even if I'm not the one making the plan,
I don't know what the plan is, and I'm
pretty sure it will end in total failure.

Raven showed me the note she was holding.

Graysen Foxx, Raven Ransom, Klart Kirby,
and Maya and Jack Delgado have my
permission to go to the junior high library.
Sincerely,
Amy Hall
Ordinary Elementary Librarian

"How did you get this?" I asked. "You didn't tell her—"

"I didn't need to," Raven said. "The minute I said you were in trouble, she asked what she could do to help. She never believed you would have failed to return all those books."

"She's the best librarian ever," Klart said. "There's no one else I'd rather have covering my back."

That was something we could all agree on. I turned to Jack and Maya. "It might be safer for you two to wait back in your classroom. We have no idea who might be watching, and the three of us could at least pass for seventh graders. But if you two come along, it's going to be obvious you're too young."

Maya put her hands on her hips. "We're getting in with a note from our elementary school librarian that says we're going to the library. Trust me, if anyone's watching, they won't have any trouble figuring out what we're doing."

Jack whispered to Maya. "I agree," she said. "Nobody would believe Raven and Gray are in junior high. Especially if Gray brings his elastic sticky hand."

"Thanks a lot," I said.

I didn't like it, but the twins had that stubborn look that said it would be easier to talk a first grader in gym class into coming out from under the rainbow parachute than it would be to talk Maya and Jack out of going with us. "Okay but keep an eye out. If you sense even a hint of trouble, get out of here."

They both saluted and formed on our flanks.

I worried that someone might question the authenticity of our note and stop us at the border, but the woman behind the counter barely glanced at it before handing it back and pushing the button that buzzed us into new territory.

There was no going back now. Would the locals notice our small statures or strange accents and turn on us as intruders? Would we be disoriented by the dizzying array of intersecting hallways and end up lost in a foreign language class none of us could understand? If we got hungry, would our stomachs be able to adjust to the unfamiliar dishes? Only time would tell.

"You know," Raven said as we trekked deep into the bowels of the building. "Maya's right. The sticky hand and fedora do make you kind of stand out, Gray."

I patted my trusty elastic friend. It had been by my side through more dicey situations than a kite in a hurricane. And without my fedora, I wouldn't feel like a real treasure hunter. You might as well ask the Doodler to give up drawing.

"It's fine," I said. "People will just think it's a really awesome Halloween costume."

Klart coughed into his fist. "Yeah, that's not really how things work on this side of the parking lot. Look around."

We'd managed to arrive just as kids were getting out of one class and heading to another. All up and down the halls that were at least twice as wide as ours, boys and girls were packed shoulder-to-shoulder like a school of mackerel in a fishing net. Kids laughed, chattered, and shouted to one

another as lockers banged open and shut. But from what I could see, not one of them was wearing so much as a set of fake Dracula fangs.

It was like we'd entered one of those dystopian societies where everyone walked the same way, talked the same talk, and no one was allowed to stand out from the others.

"What's wrong with these kids?" Maya asked. "Don't they know what time of year it is?"

"It's not that," Klart said, hunching his shoulders as he cast anxious glances around him. He was probably realizing this would be him in another year. "It's just that the worst thing a junior high student can imagine is seeming uncool. They'll do almost anything to avoid being accused of doing 'baby stuff.' So, you know, pretty much everything fun."

I shuddered. These kids had gone from the Venerable but Quick-Tempered Order of the Sixth Graders to *this*? How the mighty had fallen. If this was going to be my fate, maybe repeating fifth grade again wouldn't be so bad.

Klart puffed his cheeks and blew out a long breath. "I've heard it gets better in high school. But that might just be something adults say to keep us from abandoning all hope."

"Okay, fine," I said, taking off my hat and sticky hand and hiding them in my pack. "I just hope I don't encounter a badly angled ray of sunlight or have an important document suddenly get blown away by a stray gust of wind."

Raven smirked. "Yeah, I can see where that would be a pretty big concern—inside a school."

Nobody appreciated the sacrifices I made for the sake of the mission.

"So," Maya asked. "How do we blend in?"

"It's all about the attitude," Klart said. "Mess up your hair and wrinkle your clothes like you rolled out of bed five minutes before the first bell. Curl your upper lip like everything around you is totally dumb. And only speak in one- or two-word sentences, like 'whatever,' or 'valid,' or 'I guess.'"

Raven balled the end of one of her sleeves in her fist, pushed her hair up, and sneered. "Whatever."

Maya nodded. "Valid."

"I wish we had lockers at our school," I said, admiring the rows of numbered metal doors.

"Why?" Raven asked. "They're just cubbies with combinations you have to memorize." She looked at Klart. "I guess."

"Whatever," Klart agreed.

"Yeah. But they're way bigger and they lock. Think of all the treasure-hunting equipment you could store in them."

"Yeah," Klart said. "I'm guessing that's not such a big priority for these kids."

"Their loss," I said, reaching up to tug down the brim of my fedora before remembering I wasn't wearing it.

"Library's up there," Klart said, pointing to a wall of floor-to-ceiling windows at the top of a staircase at the end of the hall. "You're sure we can find out where the Illuminerdy's base of operations is?"

I nodded. "The junior high library has a set of property

records going back to the mid-1800s. I used it in third grade to locate the owner of a ballpoint pen circa 1987."

Raven snorted as we reached the top of the stairs. "I don't know whether to be impressed or feel sorry for you."

Klart pulled open the library door. "There's no rule that says you can't do both."

"Good point."

"All right," I said, ignoring their juvenile humor. "The property records are over—"

"Shh," Raven hissed. She pulled us together in a half-circle and dropped her voice. "Causally turn and look at the kid who just walked in. Didn't he pass us a few minutes ago in the hallway?"

I peeked in that direction out of the corner of my eye. It was a tall, skinny boy with braces. "Um, maybe?"

Klart frowned. "What should we do?"

"Let's rush him," Raven suggested. "There are three of us, and he looks like one good slug to the gut would fold him over like a chicken taco."

"No," Maya said, horrified.

"We aren't slugging anyone," I agreed. "For all we know, he's just here to get a book. See? He's going over to ask the librarian where to find it."

Raven curled her upper lip. "Or he's going over to ask her if she knows what *we're* looking for."

"How do we find out?" Klart asked.

"I've got an idea," I said, taking a pen out of my pocket. "Hold out your hands."

Carefully, I wrote the reference number for property records on each of their palms. "The three of us will split up. If he follows you, lead him to the opposite side of the library. If not, meet here."

"I like it," Maya said. "It's easy and doesn't involve trying to fold someone like a taco."

Raven shrugged. "I guess."

Trying not to seem suspicious, I wandered casually around a rack of young adult paperbacks, checked out a display of Arctic-explorer biographies, and glanced toward the front desk. The tall boy wasn't there anymore. But he wasn't following me either.

I quickly ducked into an aisle and headed to the reference section where Klart, Raven, and the twins were waiting. "Any problems?"

"We don't have to worry about him," Raven said.

I gave a sigh of relief. "He didn't follow you?"

She shook her head. "I followed him to the other side of the library, where there are these little meeting rooms with soundproof metal doors. I asked him if he could get a book for me from the top shelf next to one of the doors. When he reached up for it, I shoved him into the room and blocked the door with a chair."

"What?" I cried, turning to go let him out.

"I'm kidding," Raven said. "But it's still a good plan to keep in mind if things go south."

Wondering if I'd unleashed a monster, I opened the property records and searched the index for Sullivan. "Okay,

I've got something," I said. "According to this, they own a 23,000-square-foot house at 124 South Cherry Tree Lane."

Klart hurried to a nearby computer and pulled up the address in Google Maps. "Now that's what I call a lair!"

We all stared at the enormous mansion on the screen.

"Okay," Maya said. "That definitely looks like the place. What do we do now?"

"Fight fire with fire," Raven said with an evil laugh.

Jack whispered to Maya with a worried expression.

"No, Raven wasn't talking about a real fire." She looked at Raven. "Were you?"

"Of course not," Raven said. "But they might wish I had after we're through with them."

"They'll have all kinds of security," I said.

Raven nodded. "Which just means they'll never be expecting us."

CHAPTER 25

The Curse of Ordinary Elementary

Being a kid means accidentally knocking over houseplants, clogging the toilet, messing up the computer, and spilling cereal. Being a kid who is friends with Raven Ransom means doing all of those same things—but on purpose.

On Saturday, Halloween morning, the five of us hid in the bushes outside the Sullivan mansion.

"Does everyone remember their assignments?" Raven asked.

Jack whispered to Maya.

"On your signal, Jack sneaks through the front door, unlocks the side door for the rest of us to enter, then starts tipping over every houseplant he can find."

Klart held out a USB drive. "I shut down the firewall and use one of their computers to go to a bunch of really spammy websites so the network gets attacked by viruses."

Maya checked a cheat sheet in her palm. "I take all the

boxes of cereal out of the kitchen and dump them into their beds and dresser drawers, then soak their socks in water and stick them in the freezer."

Raven turned to me. "Gray?"

"I plug all the toilets, then bend the handles so they keep trying to flush." I rolled my eyes. "You know that even if we manage to pull off half of this, all it's going to do is get us arrested."

"That's what I'm counting on," Raven said. "The minute they threaten to call the police, I launch *Plan B*."

I frowned. "Which is?"

Raven raised one finger. "Hold that thought. Here comes our first diversion."

A van with a picture of a giant pizza on the side made its way up the white gravel driveway to the front of the mansion.

"Wait," I said. "Isn't that the same company who brought me—"

Raven nodded. "They already had Principal Redbeard's credit card number on file. All I had to do was call them again and say I had another order. A *really* big one."

Three teenagers hopped out of the van, opened the back doors, and began carrying the boxes to the front porch. One of them rang the doorbell and a girl with blonde hair answered. I pointed. "That's Rory. She's one of the kids I saw with Principal Redbeard."

"Makes sense," Klart said. "This is probably where they start their training. Like Xavier's School for Gifted Youngsters in X-Men."

The girl looked at the boxes and shook her head. But the guys with the pizzas held up a receipt and kept bringing more boxes.

Maya laughed. "Looks like they're going to have an amazing pizza party."

"The goats can probably eat some of it," Raven said as a cattle truck pulled up behind the pizza van.

A grizzled man in a cowboy hat and jeans hopped out of the truck and checked a piece of paper in his hand. "You just want me to let 'em out here? The front lawn doesn't look like it needs cutting, but these critters will definitely eat what's there."

When no one answered him, one of the pizza guys looked back and shrugged. "Sounds okay to me."

"Good enough." The cowboy unlocked the back of his truck and dozens of goats jumped out, bleating and hopping as they ripped out chunks of the perfect green sod in front of the mansion.

"How did you get those?" I asked.

Raven shrugged. "I just Googled goats."

On the front porch, Principal Redbeard pushed the pizza guys aside and ran into the front yard.

"What are you doing to my lawn!" he screamed, trying to avoid the goats who seemed to think he was the perfect target for butting into.

Raven checked her watch. "Right about now we should see—"

From the other side of the yard, a group of little kids ran across the grass and disappeared behind the house. The one in front was wearing a suit and the kid behind him had unmistakable curly brown hair.

"That's Cam and Asher."

Raven nodded. "I told them to have the first graders find all the chocolate pudding powder in their houses and dump it into the pool. The mariachi band will be here any minute. But I think Jack can go in now."

Jack saluted, then turned and raced toward the front of the house, hiding behind the pizza truck until the coast was clear. Principal Redbeard was so busy arguing with the pizza delivery people and trying not to get hit by the goats that he didn't notice Jack slipping through the front door—not even when Jack paused to open a box and grab a couple of slices of pizza before disappearing into the house.

"Follow me," Raven said, leading us past a fountain to the side of the mansion.

"How do you know your way around?" I asked.

"Google maps," she said with an evil grin.

Behind us, the Second-Grade Spy Network showed up wearing costumes from *Man of La Mancha*, the play our school had done the year before, while playing lively Latin music on their kazoos.

Klart paused and began tapping his feet. "They sound pretty good."

"Keep moving," Raven ordered.

By the time we reached the side of the house, the door was already open, and a trail of scattered dirt and tipped-over plants made it clear that Jack was doing his part.

"I'll find the cereal," Maya said, hurrying down the hall and taking a left.

"I see a computer," Klart said, disappearing into an office to the right.

"What are you going to do?" I asked Raven.

She pulled out a small camera on a strap and attached it to her head. "Set off the fire alarm to create more confusion and try to dig up as much incriminating evidence as I can find. Now go plug some toilets."

I'd never seen a house with so many bathrooms before. For the next ten minutes, I moved from one toilet to the next, clogging them with toilet paper, bottles of hand soap, towels, and anything else I could find, then opening the back of the tanks and bending the handle wire to keep the water running.

Things seemed to be getting worse outside. Kids ran through the house shouting about goats, pizza, and Latin music.

"Who knocked over the plant outside my room and

why is there Raisin Bran is my bed?" yelled a boy as the house alarm brayed on and off.

"No clue," called a girl. "But there's water running out the door of my bathroom and a bunch of little kids just dumped something into the pool out back. Now the water looks like chocolate pudding."

"Hey," another voice shouted. "What's going on with the network? How am I supposed to get any studying done when ads for back-hair removal keep popping up on the screen?"

As I stepped out of the bathroom where I'd just finished sabotaging another toilet, a girl ran past me, stopped, then turned around. "Aren't you the kid who refused to join us the other night? What are you doing here?"

It was Ann, the girl who reprogrammed the whiteboards in the math room during her test. I looked around, trying to come up with a good excuse. "I, um, changed my mind. So here I am, ready to get my—"

She glanced behind me at the water running out from the bathroom door and grabbed my shirt. "You're the reason the toilets are all overflowing."

Two girls came down the hall dragging Maya, who was still holding a box of Captain Crunch. "We found this girl putting cereal in our sheets and trying to steal our socks."

A group of teens stumbled down the stairs, trying to hold onto Jack, who was twisting and turning like an eel on a Slip 'N Slide as dirt and leaves drifted to the carpet around him. "We don't know who this kid is. He won't say anything, but we found him in the theater eating popcorn and watching *Phineas and Ferb*."

Principal Redbeard marched into the entryway, dragging Klart by the arm. "Does anyone know this intruder? I found him playing Rocket League in my office and—" He stopped and stared at me, eyes going wide.

"You!"

"*Me*," I said.

"What are you doing here?" he demanded.

I nodded at the water running out of the bathroom behind me and the Boston fern lying on the floor. "What does it look like?"

"I suppose you've changed your mind and want to join the Illuminerdy? Did you seriously think you could force your way in by making fake pizza deliveries and knocking over house plants?"

Maya giggled. "Wait until you try to change your socks."

"Big mistake," said the girl who had introduced herself to me as a doctor.

Principal Redbeard shoved Klart forward. "I'm calling the police and having you all arrested for trespassing, vandalism, damage to property—"

"Then we'll have you charged with computer fraud," Raven said, stepping out from behind a statue. "Hacking, changing school records, illegally accessing a government network."

Principal Redbeard frowned. "Who are you?"

"The person who is going to expose your group and get

you arrested for messing with my friend." Raven grinned. "Trust me, hacking into a school computer, changing a student's records, and altering financial documents are way bigger crimes than delivering goats and clogging toilets."

"You don't have proof we did any of that stuff," said one of the boys holding Jack.

"Every single time you hacked the school system, you left a trail," Klart said.

"There isn't any trail," Ann said, still holding my arm. "I removed all of the evidence before I logged out—I mean, hypothetically."

Raven nodded. "That's true. But the hack I did to watch the school network stored a record of everything you did."

"I thought you deleted that," I said.

Raven shrugged. "I was going to. I just hadn't gotten around to it yet."

Principal Redbeard chuckled. "Good luck proving that the hack originated here. We use data encryption even the government doesn't know about yet."

"They do now." Raven tapped the camera strapped to her forehead. "I'm streaming this entire conversation straight to the internet, and what you just said sounds a lot like a confession to me."

For a moment every single person went silent. Then Klart, Raven, Maya, Jack, and I burst into laughter. I yanked my arm free from the girl holding it. "Welcome to the *Curse of Ordinary Elementary*."

CHAPTER 26
A Battle of Wits

An experienced treasure hunter has to be prepared for anything. Basic tools include a compass, field journal, grappling hook, shovel, map, and a flashlight. But sometimes, the only tool that matters is the one inside your head.

"What's all that commotion?" asked a white-haired old man as he rolled his electric wheelchair to the second-floor railing and glared down at us. "I was trying to sleep."

Maya looked up and gasped. "It's the scary old man from the painting."

She was right. It did look just like the man in the portrait we'd found.

"You can't be Howard Sullivan the Third," Klart said. "There's no way he can still be alive."

"Don't be rude," Principal Redbeard growled.

But the old man just laughed. "Sometimes I wonder how *I'm* still alive. But, no, I'm not Howard. I'm his grandson, Hubert."

"You won the spelling bee and scratched the Illuminerdy symbol into the back," I said.

He turned to me, pointing a knobby finger. "And you must be Graysen Foxx, the boy who found it. I hid my medal below the stage when I was just a lad—along with the painting of my grandfather—as part of a game for some friends of mine. I had no idea it would take almost a hundred years for someone to find it."

"You should have told me it was there and saved us all the trouble of having to get it back," Principal Redbeard muttered. "That was a serious security risk."

The old man snorted and tugged at the plastic tube running from the oxygen tank on his wheelchair into his nose. "Now you're the one being rude, Sylvester. No one would have given a flying fiddle about that old medal if you hadn't made such a fuss about it."

He wheeled closer to look down at me. "I suppose that

would also make you the most recent student to solve my puzzle. Congratulations, and welcome to the Illuminerdy."

I pushed up my fedora. "Actually, sir, all five of us solved it. Me and my four friends."

"Well now," he said with a sandy-sounding laugh. "Then congratulations and welcome to all five of you."

Principal Redbeard shook his head. "That's a lie. He was the only one to solve the five-door puzzle. And he's not a member because he rejected our offer, incurring the Curse of the Illuminerdy. Now it appears that he and his friends are trying to blackmail their way in by vandalizing our house."

Raven raised her fist. "We didn't come here to join your pathetic club. We came here to force you to stop attacking our friend. And to tell the rest of the world who you really are and what you're doing."

She stepped forward to make sure her camera got a nice, close image, but Principal Redbeard yanked it off her head, threw it to the floor, and stomped on it.

"Leave her alone!" I yelled, grabbing his beard and pulling him away from her.

"Let go of our leader," one of the kids snarled. Three of the boys jumped on me, pinning my arms and pushing me to the ground.

"Stop that," the old man called.

Maya kicked one of the boys in the shin, while Klart jumped onto another boy's back, pulling his hair and riding him like a rodeo bull.

Upstairs, an airhorn split the air. We all stopped to

look up at the old man. "Stop this at once, or I'll have you all thrown into the pool, which currently looks like a backed-up sewer."

When we'd all released each other and stepped away, Hubert Sullivan nodded. "I'm coming downstairs to sort this all out." He sniffed the air. "Get things cleaned up and bring some of that pizza I smell. I'm hungry."

Michael, the red-haired boy with the missing front teeth, shook his head. "It's not even nine in the morning. Don't you want breakfast?"

"I've always thought they got foods wrong," Mr. Sullivan said. "Pizza is the perfect morning meal—bread, cheese, sauce, and meat. Waffles and eggs are really more an evening fare. Now, assemble in the dining room."

• • •

"Let me see if I've got the timeline right," the old man said, finishing his second slice of pizza and wiping sauce off his chin with a napkin. "You and your friends found my spelling bee medal and deciphered the message on it, beginning the Illuminerdy test."

"We actually read it off of the ring in your grandfather's portrait," I said. "Because Michael stole the medal from me."

Michael nodded with his gapped-tooth grin.

"But the medal was what sent us to the trophy case, where we found out about you."

"I see," Hubert said. "Then you turned the bell, climbed the card catalog, solved the math puzzles, rode the projector carts, and chose the correct door. All in less time than any of the other children we've tested."

"Yes, sir."

He tented his hands together in front of his face. "But when my grandson, Sylvester, offered to let you join the Illuminerdy, you turned him down—even though he told you that doing so would result in being cursed?"

I nodded.

He studied me with a puzzled expression. "Weren't you interested in the opportunity our group offers?"

"Oh, I totally was," I said. "It sounds amazing. But my friends and I promised each other that if we found the treasure, we'd split it. And I never would have completed the quest if it wasn't for them. If I deserve to be here, so do they."

Hubert took a third slice of pizza, then put it back. "When I was your age, I could eat an entire pizza. But I'm afraid my stomach isn't what it used to be." He looked at Jack, Maya, Klart, and Raven. "This morning the five of you came here trying to force us to remove the curse from Graysen."

"No," Raven said. "We came here to show you what being cursed feels like."

"Point taken." The old man turned to the Illuminerdy members gathered around the table. "I'd say they succeeded, wouldn't you?"

The kids all nodded, muttering about broken toilets and frozen socks.

Principal Redbeard stood and crossed his arms. "We've

never removed the Curse of the Illuminerdy before and we won't now. It sets a dangerous example."

"We're not removing *our* curse either," Raven said.

Mr. Sullivan tapped his fingers on the table. "I only see one way to resolve this."

"The courts?" Principal Redbeard asked. "I can call our attorneys."

"Continue to attack each other until one side gives up?" Raven asked.

"I know someone with a llama farm," Klart said.

"No," the old man growled. "This began with a test of intelligence. The only way to end it is with a battle of wits. Your smartest champion versus the Illuminerdy's smartest champion, head-to-head."

Principal Redbeard and the rest of the Illuminerdy looked at me with gloating smiles that made it clear who they thought would win.

Klart cracked his knuckles, Raven rubbed her lips, and even the twins appeared nervous.

"Fine," I said. "I accept your brain-power battle. But instead of having the test be one-on-one, let's make it five-on-five. Your five best against me and my friends."

"That doesn't seem like it would help you," Mr. Sullivan said. "The Illuminerdy are made up of the most brilliant minds in the world, but you are the only one of your friends to pass the test."

"Maybe," I said. "But solving problems isn't about having a high IQ. It's about trust, friendship, and working together. I didn't just refuse your offer because it didn't include my friends, I turned you down because I think you're doing things the wrong way."

The old man frowned. "How so?"

"Instead of spending all your money on only a few kids who pass your tests, why not invest in kids who might be smart in different ways—who might not even know what they're capable of until they get the chance?"

Principal Redbeard guffawed. "That kind of thinking is the whole reason I left the school system. Average students are more interested in playing with toys than they are with learning."

Jack whispered to his sister and Maya snorted. "If that's what you think, then it's a good thing you left. You were probably a horrible principal."

"Take it or leave it," I said. "We either battle you five-on-five or not at all."

"We accept your challenge," Principal Redbeard said with a sneer. "Our five best versus you and your . . . *friends*. If you win—which you won't—we agree to remove our curse. But when you lose—which you absolutely will—not only do you keep the curse, but your four friends get cursed as well."

Klart shook his head, trying to get my attention. But I was as annoyed as a kid who can't find the last answer in a word search puzzle.

I tugged my fedora low over my eyes. "You want to up the stakes? Let's make it interesting. When we win—which

we will the same way we beat your last puzzle, together—
you agree to stop spending all of your money on only the
smartest kids and try giving it to *all* kids instead."

Principal Redbeard looked at his grandfather, but the
old man simply looked on.

"Okay." The principal rubbed his beard. "But know
this. When our team defeats you and your *average* friends,
I will purchase Ordinary Elementary, kick out every single
student, teacher, and staff member, and turn it into a private
school for only the smartest kids in the world."

CHAPTER 27
Teamwork

The Illuminerdy might have more money, higher test scores, more experience, and a better education. But there was one thing they didn't have: the best friends in the world. I liked those odds just fine.

"No offense," Klart said as we followed Hubert Sullivan's wheelchair to go over the rules of the battle of wits. "But for a smart kid, agreeing to their contest was a really dumb idea."

"You think we're going to lose?" I asked.

He sighed. "In a video game contest, sure. In an obstacle course, definitely. We could probably beat them in ping pong, eighties trivia, octopus juggling, Monopoly, or even jousting if the lances weren't too heavy. But in a battle of wits? Let's just say, I'm pretty sure we're all going to get cursed. I'm not looking forward to having to repeat sixth grade because of unpaid library fees."

"Gray wouldn't have said yes unless he had a plan." Maya looked up at me. "You *do* have a plan, don't you?"

I opened my mouth.

"We're going to cheat, right?" Raven whispered.

I slowed, letting the old man get a little ahead of us. "What are you talking about?"

"Bending the rules," Raven said. "Bribing a judge. Spying on the other team to figure out their plans. Stealing their supplies. That's how the world works. Tesla invented the light bulb before Thomas Edison, but Edison got the patent because he superglued Tesla's pants to his chair. These kids might be smart, but the devious shall prevail."

Klart smiled. "Okay, I'm starting to feel better about our chances."

I shook my head. "I'm pretty sure superglue was invented *after* the light bulb. And even if Edison did get the patent, *we're* not cheating. We're just going to beat them at their own game."

"How?" Maya asked. "You heard Principal Redbeard. Being super intelligent is what got those kids here in the first place. They probably train for brain battles every day."

Klart nodded. "Face it. We might be some of the smartest kids in our school, but compared to the Illuminerdy, we're all kinds of mediocre."

"Speak for yourself," Raven said. "I may not have as high an IQ as some of those kids, but in other ways I'm freaking brilliant."

"Good point," I said. "You're great at strategy, Klart is incredible at math, Maya is amazing at logic and riddles, and Jack has an awesome imagination. We got through the quest, didn't we?"

Jack whispered to Maya. "He says that *you're* the only one who got through the whole quest. And even you nearly didn't. What if I hadn't mentioned the painting? Or if Jack hadn't been wearing his night vision goggles? What if you didn't know about card catalogs, or Klart didn't know about math, or Raven didn't go back for the abacus? We only made it as far as we did because we were lucky."

"It wasn't luck," I said. "It was teamwork. Yes, you thought of looking at the painting. And it was a great idea. But it only worked because I listened to you. Then when I noticed the angle of Mr. Sullivan's head, Jack believed in me enough to climb up the roof to the bell tower and unlock the door for us."

Klart rubbed his chin. "I wouldn't have made it to the math room if I hadn't followed Raven through the vents."

"And I wouldn't have gone back for the abacus," Raven said, "if it wasn't for Klart showing me how to use Napier's Bones and Graysen explaining that the puzzles that look the easiest are sometimes the hardest."

"Exactly." I unsnapped my sticky hand, bobbing it up and down. "Everybody hears about the big-name inventors and thinkers and philosophers. But none of those people could have done what they did without thousands of people who had ideas before them. Individually, those kids might be smarter than us, but together, we're unstoppable. So what do you all say?"

Klart gave a sideways grin. "I mean, it's not like we have much choice at this point. But sure, I'm in."

"I'd feel better if we had the Second-Grade Spy Network on our side," Raven said. "But, yeah, let's do it."

Maya folded her arms. "Do you really think we can win this, Gray?"

I nodded, hoping I was right. "I do."

"Okay," she said. "I believe in you."

Jack whispered in her ear and Maya smiled. "Jack says he's with you to the end. Unless it's for sure that we're going to lose. Then, he'll probably sneak out."

Ahead of us, the dark wooden doors to the library automatically swung open, and Mr. Sullivan wheeled his chair into an enormous library filled with more books than even the junior high.

The Illuminerdy team—Carter, Ann, Samantha, Michael, and Rory—were waiting in front of a high-tech video display when we got there.

"Carter Stevens," said the boy who'd first met me when I finished the quest. "Engineer."

"Rory Roberts," said the blonde girl. "Historical linguist and best-selling author."

"Great to meet you," Klart said, shaking everyone's hands. "Klart Kirby, gamer, recently ex-second-in-command to the Doodler, and possibly soon-to-be repeat sixth grader."

The Illuminerdy kids looked at him like they weren't sure whether he was joking or not, and Rory moved back a few steps as if she thought he might be contagious.

"This contest is quite simple," Mr. Sullivan said, turning his wheelchair to face us.

"Please let it be an academic decathlon," Michael said, his eyes gleaming.

"A robotics war," Ann whispered.

Jack mouthed something that looked like *Pokémon battle.*

The old man pushed a button on the arm of his chair and an image of a locked metal door with a five-number digital combination appeared on the display behind him.

"Lock picking," Raven said. "My specialty."

Dr. Ferriera sniffed. "How . . . *charming.*"

Hubert ignored everyone's comments and tapped the arm of his chair again, revealing a diagram of a large room divided into five sections. "Each team will enter an identical room consisting of five puzzles and a steel exit door."

"An escape room?" Principal Redbeard asked. "Isn't that a bit childish?"

"I'm all about childish stuff," Klart said. "Laser tag, mini golf, go-karts."

Principal Redbeard grimaced. "When you suggested a battle of wits, I assumed you were talking about something more like—"

"It's not an escape room. It's a puzzle room!" Hubert Sullivan snapped. "And it's not open for debate."

He continued, showing a series of images on the screen. "Each room contains a series of five puzzles requiring knowledge from various arts and sciences. After entering the puzzle room, the way out will be sealed by a solid steel door with a magnetic lock."

"Sounds like an escape room to me," Rory muttered.

Hubert glared at her. "To open the lock, you must enter a five-digit code which will be obtained by—"

"Solving the puzzles," Carter said. "We get it."

The old man nodded with a sour expression like he was wondering if he really wanted the bossy Illuminerdy kids to win after all. "Each puzzle will provide you with one digit of the code. But if you enter a digit wrong, all puzzles in your room will be locked for fifteen minutes."

Klart leaned toward Raven. "What kind of house has built-in escape rooms?"

"The kind of house where brainiacs take IQ tests for kicks and giggles," Raven muttered.

Hubert Sullivan slammed his hand against the arm of his wheelchair. "Quiet!"

Everyone stopped whispering and stared at him.

"The next person who says a word without being called upon will be turned over to the authorities as a trespasser and banned from this house permanently. That includes you, Sylvester. Do I make myself clear?"

We all nodded silently, including Principal Redbeard.

"Very well. The two rooms are identical and separated by a clear wall, which means you can each see the other team's progress. So be careful about what you give away. The door locks are set into the wall so that the other team can't see what code you are entering. But the lights above them flash green or red so you can each tell how many digits the others have solved. Any questions?"

Raven raised her hand. "What are the rules?"

"Simple. The first team to unlock the door and leave the room wins."

Jack whispered to Maya.

Hubert cocked his head. "Does the silent child have a question?"

Maya swallowed. "He, um, wants to know if we'll be done before dark, so he can go trick-or-treating."

The Illuminerdy kids laughed, but the old man didn't seem to be amused. His blue eyes glinted as icily as the portrait of his grandfather. "I imagine this contest will be over much quicker than you expect."

CHAPTER 28
A Bridge to Nowhere

When the stakes are high and your back
is against the wall, you have to know who
you can trust. If I had to choose between
geniuses with an engineering degree and
third graders with a popsicle stick plan,
I'd pick the Delgado twins every time.

"What kind of puzzles do you think they'll be?" Maya whispered as we walked toward the escape rooms.

"I'm hoping for Rocket League," Klart said.

Jack snickered.

"Whatever they are, the key is to solve them together," I said. "Each of those Illuminerdy kids is used to being the best. I'm guessing they don't have much experience working together. But we're used to being a team, so let's just make sure we listen to each other and—"

"You're thinking about what I did in the math room, aren't you?" Raven asked.

"No." I shook my head. But I kind of was—at least a little. Mr. Sullivan had said that entering a wrong number into the lock would freeze the game for fifteen minutes. If any one of us decided to try to win the game on our own and got the answer wrong, it could mean the difference between helping thousands of kids and being kicked out of our own school.

Raven put her hands on her hips. "If you don't trust me, just say so, and I'll leave now."

I shook my head. "We can't do this without you."

"You're the only reason we're here," Klart added. "So, thanks, I guess."

Jack whispered to Maya.

She looked from him to Raven.

"Well?" Raven asked.

"He, um, says that he doesn't trust you. But he trusts you."

Raven removed her hands from her hips and laughed. "I actually completely understand that. Thanks."

Jack nodded.

"Let's get this over with," Dr. Samantha Ferrier said. "I have to get to the hospital and make rounds."

Hubert Sullivan pointed us to our doors while Principal Redbeard looked on. "May the best team win."

"Thanks," both groups said at once.

"The only place you'll win is in your dreams," Rory said. "I'll have all the problems done before you five can tie your shoes."

"You mean *I'll* have the problems done," Carter said.

"I am the engineer. You study dead languages and write books no one reads."

Rory raised an eyebrow. "I'm sure your engineering degree will come in very handy when we have to decipher—"

"Begin!" Hubert shouted and both of our doors swung open.

"Okay," Raven yelled as we all raced into the room. "Everyone spread out and—Whoa!"

We all skidded to a halt less than ten feet inside the door, where the floor of the room disappeared into a sheer chasm nearly ten feet across and fifteen feet wide. Peering over the edge into the darkness, I could just make out what looked like jagged rocks on the bottom far below.

Klart backed slowly away. "I've heard of creepy basements, but this . . ."

"That's not possible," I said. "It has to be some kind of holographic image or something."

Raven knelt and reached over the side until her whole arm was in the pit. "This is an international group of super-brains with nearly unlimited resources. You feel like testing that theory?"

I shook my head.

"What are we supposed to do with it?" Klart asked. "It's a little obvious for a bear trap."

"Who cares?" Raven said. "Let's just go around it."

"Wait!" Maya called, picking up a piece of paper from the floor to the side of the door. "To get the first number for the door and unlock the second puzzle, build a bridge strong enough to support your entire team as they cross chasm one," she read. "You may use the tools and materials provided, including the computer."

Raven snatched the paper from her hands. "Let me see that."

"It's not very poetic," Klart said. "I mean they could have called the hole something more memorable than *chasm one* like the *Drop of Death* or the *Pit of Peril.*"

"I don't think they were going for poetic," I said, studying the computer and the pile of building materials on the floor next to it. The supplies seemed to be divided into three groups: wooden boards and dowels, metal beams and brackets, and coils of cable and rope.

"Anybody know how to build a bridge?"

Klart turned on the computer. "Let me Google it." A moment later he snorted. "No internet. There's just something called *AutoCAD.*"

He clicked the icon and opened a software package filled with bridge designs. But one look at the plans made it clear that we would never be able to build any of them.

Raven glanced through the clear plastic wall to where two of the Illuminerdy kids were fighting over the computer while the rest moved around girders and cable.

I took off my hat and ran my fingers through my hair. I was a treasure hunter, not an engineer. "We're never going to be able to figure out any of that fancy stuff. Let's just nail a bunch of boards together and call it good."

"A little problem with that," Raven said. "There's no

nails or screws. And no hammer or screwdriver we could use even if there were."

"That can't be right," I said, pawing through the building supplies. "How are you supposed to put the pieces together?"

On the other side of the wall, Carter put on a tinted face mask and squeezed the handle of a machine that spit out bright blue sparks.

"They're using an arc welder to connect the metal girders," Klart said. He looked doubtfully at a big metal box with lots of gauges and hoses. "Maybe I can figure out how to use it."

Jack, who had been whispering furiously to Maya, stomped his foot.

"What's he so upset about?" I asked, wondering if he was already planning his escape.

Maya looked from her twin to the rest of us. "He says he knows how to build a bridge."

"Nothing about that kid would surprise me," Klart said. "But unless he has a screwdriver hidden in his pocket or knows how to weld, I don't—"

Jack whispered again, pointing to the piles of supplies.

"He says he doesn't need screws or a welder. He says . . ." She stared at Jack. But he nodded his head energetically. "He says he can build a bridge that will get us across the chasm using only those pieces of wood and the rope. He says it's called a Da Vinci bridge."

"Wasn't Da Vinci, like, a sculptor?" Klart asked.

"A really famous painter," I said. "But he was also a scientist and an inventor."

Jack grabbed an armful of boards and a coil of rope, neither of which looked very sturdy, and dragged them toward the hole in the floor.

I looked at Maya. She knew her brother better than anyone. "What do you think?"

Maya sighed. "He swears the bridge will work. But . . . he says he learned how to build it using popsicle sticks."

Klart gasped. "Do you want to trust your life to a third-grade popsicle stick engineer?"

Raven grabbed a pile of boards. "I do."

"You do?" I asked, following her as she carried the boards and dowels to where Jack was laying things out on the floor next to the chasm.

She dropped the supplies on the floor next to Jack and turned around to stare at me. "You said we need to trust each other. Did you mean that?"

"Sure," I said, looking at the pieces of wood that seemed especially thin next to the enormous opening of the chasm. "But—"

"No buts!" she shouted, cutting me off. She pointed to where the Illuminerdy kids were holding up a metal frame as Carter welded the pieces together. "Those kids are smarter than us. They're going to solve this problem, and the next one, and the next one, and the one after that. So we can either trust each other and work together beginning right now, or we can give up before we ever start."

I looked from her to Klart to Maya. She'd just used my own words against me—how could I argue with that? "Okay, let's do it."

Five minutes later, Raven, Klart, and I lifted the last piece of wood as Jack and Maya shoved the final dowel into place. It was a strange-looking contraption, with boards going over and under dowels. Somehow all the pieces supported each other and stayed in place with only their own weight and some knotted rope.

Looking at our finished bridge, I wasn't entirely sure if the design was brilliant or if it was all going to fall apart the minute we put our weight on it. But Raven and Klart lifted one end as Maya, Jack, and I lifted the other. Together we carried the bridge around one side of the opening and centered it on the pit in the floor. Finally, we set it down, forming an arch across the chasm.

On the other side of the transparent wall, the Illumi-nerdy kids were nearly done welding something that looked

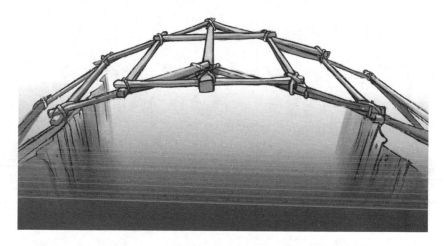

like it could hold the weight of an elephant. One of them turned in our direction and pointed. Soon all of them were pointing at us and laughing.

All except Carter. He pulled off his face shield and stared.

One by one, the rest of their group lowered their fingers, their expressions changing from laughter to worry.

I turned to see what they were looking at and found Jack, Maya, Raven, and Klart all perched on top of the bridge.

Raven smirked. "Are you coming?"

CHAPTER 29
The Music Room

I may not know much about music, but I know what I like. This definitely wasn't it.

The minute we stepped off the bridge onto the other side of the chasm, a metal tile dropped from the ceiling onto the floor with a clang.

Raven snatched it up. "Six," she whispered, looking over at the Illuminerdy kids who were rushing to drag their bridge to the chasm.

Jack and Maya raced back to the door to enter the first number of the code, while Klart, Raven, and I watched.

"I think we might actually be able to beat them," Klart said.

"Don't get too confident," Raven said. "We haven't won this yet." She looked at me, and I could tell she was thinking about all the times she'd swooped in at the last second to take a treasure away from me.

Jack pushed the six on the lock. Now the Illuminerdy kids were watching too. They shouted angrily as the first light above our door turned green.

At the same time, a section of the wall in front of us slid aside, revealing . . .

"Music?" Raven asked as we walked into a room filled with more musical instruments than I knew existed. It was packed with everything: from pianos to stringed instruments, woodwinds to drums, even including a xylophone big enough for a class party to eat their pizza on. "I thought this was supposed to be an intelligence test."

"Musical talent is totally a sign of high intelligence," Klart said, running his hand across a table filled with bells, cymbals, and chimes. "In fact, math and music actually have a lot in common."

Raven smirked. "You don't happen to be a musician, do you?"

Klart blushed. "My mom might be a violin teacher. And I might be working on forming a ska band called the Shrieking Paladins. But that has nothing to do with the fact that experts have done tons of studies linking a love of music to being smart."

Jack ran into the room, spotted the giant xylophone, and pounded the bars with the wooden mallet as he danced from one foot to the other.

Klart shrugged. "Those studies might not be 100 percent accurate."

"So, what's next?" Maya asked, pushing her hair out of her face.

Raven went to a metal stand at the front of the room

and picked up a sheet of music. "Maybe it has something to do with this?"

"Let me see it," Klart said. He looked at the music, turned the sheet over, and frowned.

On the other side of the clear wall, the Illuminerdy kids raced into their music room, saw Klart holding the sheet, and ran to their stand to get the music.

"Quick, play it before they do," Raven said.

In the other room, Michael and Ann argued over the music before Ann finally took the sheet and ran to the nearest piano.

Klart leaned his shoulder against the clear wall with an odd smile. "This should be interesting."

"What's the matter?" I asked. "Can't you play it?"

"No," Klart said, not looking especially worried. "But I'm pretty sure she can't either."

We all turned to watch the Illuminerdy girl sit down at the piano, open the keyboard cover, place the music in front of her, and frown.

"What's she doing?" I asked.

"Trying to read it," Klart said. "Unless she's spent a lot of time around music, she probably doesn't know what she's looking at."

After reaching toward the keys several times and stopping, Ann shook her head. The other Illuminerdy kids surrounded her, shouting and pointing at the piano.

Raven clenched her fists. "Why are we just watching? They're going to figure out how to play it eventually."

"Not on that piano."

"Why not?" I asked.

Klart laughed. "Because it isn't piano music. In fact, it can't be played on any one instrument at all."

The kid sounded as off balance as a three-legged piano bench, but he seemed to know what he was talking about. He set the piece of paper back on the stand and grabbed a book from the piano called *Twenty Great Ragtime Songs*.

"This is called musical notation," he said, opening the book to the first song. "A person who wants to play or sing a song reads the music the same way you read words on a page."

I nodded. "Historians have discovered music written on tablets that is over a thousand years old. But the first music produced on a printing press wasn't until—"

Raven scowled. "Do you really think this is the time for a history lesson?"

"Probably not," I admitted. "Go on."

Klart ran his finger across the page. "These five lines are called the staff and the circles with lines going up or down are called notes. How much the circle is filled in and how high or low it is on the staff it tells the musician what pitch to play and how long to hold it. These symbols on the left are called the clef, the key signature, and the time signature. They tell you what pitch range to play in, what key the song is in, and how fast or slow to play."

Raven bounced from one foot to the other, glancing anxiously toward the Illuminerdy kids, who were still arguing. "Can't we skip all this and just play the song on the paper?"

"See, that's the thing," Klart said. "It isn't exactly a song."

I moved around him to get a closer look at the paper. I'd taken two years of piano before my parents realized I was much better at deciphering the kinds of notes kids passed to their friends than playing the ones on a piano. But I didn't recognize anything on the page.

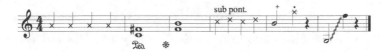

"That doesn't look like any music I've ever seen."

"Me either," Klart said. "I think they did that on purpose."

"Does that mean you can't read it?" I asked.

Klart chewed his lower lip. "I mean, I know a couple of the symbols, but the others might as well have been written by aliens."

Jack's eyes lit up.

Maya shook her head at her brother. "He said 'might as well have been' not *was*. This isn't extraterrestrial music."

I scratched my head. "What we have here is a musical mystery, a rhythmic riddle, a tuneful tes—"

Raven glared at me.

"Right. Let's approach this the way we would any other perplexing puzzle." I turned to Klart. "You said that music is like math."

"In a lot of ways, sure. The notes on the page are kind of like numbers."

"And the other notations are like math symbols," I said, feeling the same way I did when I came across an especially hard trap. "All we have to do is figure out what the notation means and solve the problem."

"Yeah," Klart said. "That makes sense."

I pulled the group together. "Everyone spread out and find all the books you can on advanced musical notation. But try not to let the Illuminerdy figure out what you're doing," I said, looking into the other room where Michael and Samantha were trying to push each other off the piano bench as they each attempted to play the keys at the same time.

Klart grabbed a pen. "I'll start taking notes."

Twenty minutes later, Klart set down the pen and wiped his forehead. "Okay, I think I've got it."

"Can you play it?" Maya asked.

"*I* can't," Klart said. "But *we* can."

Raven held up her hands. "Not me. The only musical instrument I've ever played was the triangle in third grade. And I stunk."

"We don't have any choice," Klart said. "The music is written for several different instruments. The only way to perform it is as a group."

"I played one of those little-kid violins in first grade," Maya said. Jack whispered to her, and she added, "He says he always wanted to play the drums."

"Great," Klart said. "Jack, go over to that drums set. But

don't hit anything until I show you. Maya, grab a violin. Graysen, you go over to the xylophone, and Raven, grab a trumpet. Also see if you can find a toilet plunger. Preferably one that hasn't been in a toilet."

Raven shook her head, her face so pale that each of her freckles stood out like one of those dot-to-dot puzzles where you connected the numbers to draw a giraffe wearing a tie.

I patted her on the back. "Trust each other, remember?"

"I do," she said, her jaw clenched. "It's me I don't trust. I don't want to mess this up." She shook her head. "You know how the kindergartners always do a little musical show at the end of the year?"

I nodded.

"And you know how there's always one kid who's always behind everyone else?"

"Yeah . . ."

"I was that kid," she said. "Only I was so far behind that I was still being a teapot pouring out my spout while the rest of kids were singing about Old MacDonald's farm."

"Don't worry," Klart said. "I won't let you mess up."

"You've got this," Maya said, giving Raven a fist bump.

Raven shook her head and sighed. "Fine, tell me what to do."

One by one, Klart went around to each of us, showing Maya how to hold the violin under her chin and where to put the bow, explaining to Jack which drum to hit when, and making sure I knew what to do on the xylophone.

"They're spying on us," Raven said as Klart showed her

how to hold the trumpet with
one hand and the plunger with
the other.

She was right. The
Illuminerdy kids had
stopped fighting over
the piano and were
now crowded against
the clear wall, watching
everything we did.

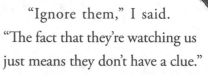

"Ignore them," I said.
"The fact that they're watching us
just means they don't have a clue."

Raven glared at the other team. "Maybe. But I'm going
to make them regret it."

"Okay," Klart said, sitting down at the piano. "Everyone
ready?"

I nodded, trying to get a grip on the wooden xylophone
mallet with my sweaty hand.

For a minute, nothing happened. Then another metal
tile fell from the ceiling.

Raven ran and picked it up. "Eight!" she shouted. "The
second number is eight."

"Shhhhh," I hissed. But it was too late. One of the Illuminerdy kids was already running to the door lock. Now they
wouldn't have to play the song we'd spent so much time figuring out.

Maya leaned in to look at the tile and frowned. "That's not an eight."

"It isn't?" Raven asked with a devious grin. She turned the tile. "Oh, wow, you're right. It's a three. I hope no one heard what I said."

From where he stood in front of his team's door, Michael grinned and waved at us. He punched the number into their lock and the light above turned red as a robotic voice blared, "*Incorrect entry. All puzzles locked for fifteen minutes.*"

Raven shrugged. "Oops!"

CHAPTER 30
The Great Escape

Every treasure hunter worth their salt knows
that finding the treasure is tough. But the pros
are the ones who understand that getting out
in one piece after you find it is even harder.

The third puzzle was a science lab where we were supposed to mix different elements to create a specific reaction. But no matter how carefully I followed the directions, every time I combined the final two beakers, nothing happened.

The Illuminerdy kids had to wait fifteen minutes to continue the music room puzzle, but because they'd been spying on us, the minute the timer beeped for them to continue, they grabbed the same instruments we had and nailed it on their first try.

"Hurry," Klart said, as the Illuminerdy raced out of the music room and into their lab.

"Don't rush me." I looked from the instructions to the experiment, making sure I had everything right. "Okay, here goes."

But when I poured the liquid from beaker into another,

making sure I had exactly the right amount, nothing happened.

"Let me," Raven said, pushing past me.

"What do you think you did wrong?" Maya asked.

"I don't know," I admitted. At least the Illuminerdy kids didn't seem to be doing any better. They were all arguing and pushing each other aside to get to the chemicals.

Maya frowned. "What if the point of the test isn't doing the experiment at all?"

"What do you mean?" I asked.

"It's like you were saying about the problems in the math room. Mixing a bunch of chemicals seems pretty easy. Which could mean that it's ⎯ "

"Really hard," I said. "Of course. How did I miss it?"

Maya grinned. "Because you were trying to do everything yourself?"

I laughed. "Good point. How would you solve this puzzle?"

She thought for a minute, then looked up at the periodic table chart above the worktable and grabbed a pen. "Have you ever seen those T-shirts that spell out words using different elements? Read me the names of the elements you've been trying to combine."

I'd tried the experiment so many times I didn't even need to look at the instructions to rattle them off. Polonium, iodine, sulfur—"

"Slow down," Maya said, looking from the chart to

what she was writing. "Okay, the chemical abbreviation for Polonium is *Po*. Iodine is *I*. What's next?

I read off the other elements as she wrote their chemical abbreviations from the periodic table. "Polonium, iodine, sulfur, oxygen, and nitrogen."

"Po-I-S-O-N. Poison."

Jack picked up a bottle with a skull and crossbones on it, and the third tile dropped from the ceiling.

"You're amazing," I said as we ran to the door to enter the third number, a four. Klart pressed the button and the third light turned green.

Maya shrugged. "Nope, just an ordinary kid helping out another ordinary kid to do extraordinary things."

"Okay," Raven said. "Just two more."

The fourth puzzle was a safe that required us to rewrite a computer program to open it. Even with Raven and Klart working together, it took longer than it should have. Meanwhile, the Illuminerdy kids hacked the safe software in seconds.

By the time Raven ran to enter the second-to-last digit— a nine—and the fourth light turned green, the Illuminerdy were right behind us.

"Hurry!" Maya shouted. "They just got the fourth number too."

We all ran to the last problem. In the middle of the room was a sculpture of a brain. Written beneath it were the words:

You have power over me.
The strength within you lies.

*The key you seek is multiplied,
by knowing my demise.*

"Please tell me that means something to you," Raven said.

"Maybe." I read the lines again. "You have power over me. The strength within you lies. Why does that seem so familiar?"

Klart snorted. "Sounds like something a politician would say."

"That's it!" I slapped him on the back. "It's a quote from the Roman emperor, Marcus Aurelius. 'You have power over your mind—not outside events. Realize this, and you will find strength.'"

Maya nodded excitedly. "That's why there's a brain, because you have power over your mind. And we can get the key by—"

"Multiplying his demise," I finished. "I know this. Marcus Aurelius was born in 121 and he died in 180. One times eight is eight. The last number to the lock is eight."

Raven ran for the door.

"That's not right," Klart said. "If he died in 180, it's one times eight times *zero*, which means the last number for the door is zero."

"Wait!" we both shouted.

But it was too late. Raven had already entered eight as the last number.

The light turned red as the robotic voice repeated its message. "*Incorrect entry. All puzzles locked for fifteen minutes.*"

Across the wall, the Illuminerdy kids looked over and cheered.

"Ha!" Carter said. "Serves you right."

"Hang on," Rory said, looking at their last puzzle. "I know what this is."

Klart glared at Raven. "Why did you enter the number so fast?"

"It's not my fault," Raven snarled. "Gray was the one who did the math wrong."

"I told you I stink at math," I said.

"Klart should have checked your answer first," Maya yelled. "Now we're going to lose."

As we all stood there blaming each other, the only one not arguing was Jack. Beside us, he turned red as he closed his eyes and scrunched up his face. Then, suddenly, with what seemed like incredible effort, he shouted, "Work together!"

We fell silent, stunned.

Raven looked from Jack to Maya. "It's not dark. How did he . . . ?"

"I don't know," Maya said. "It's the first time."

Klart stared across the wall at the Illuminerdy, who were flipping through a thick book, and patted Jack on the shoulder. "Sorry, my dude. Unless you know how to pick a lock, we're toast."

"No," I said. "Jack's right. We've made it this far together. We aren't giving up now. Does anyone have any ideas?"

Raven looked up. "Maybe."

She raced across the room and unplugged a power strip from the lab.

"What are you doing?" I asked, running after her.

"No time to explain," she puffed, grabbing another power strip. "Do you trust me?"

"Absolutely," I said at once.

"Then get every power strip you can find and take them to the door, along with anything else that runs on electricity."

"What's she doing?" Klart asked.

"No clue," I said. "But whatever it is, we need to help. Do what she said."

Racing back through the puzzles, we all grabbed every electrical item we could find and brought them back to Raven, who was stringing the power strips into one long chain. The first one in the line was plugged into an outlet next to the door.

Klart's eyes lit up. "She's trying to overload the circuits."

"Will it work?" I asked.

"Maybe," he said as we plugged in the electronics. "This house is really old."

"I've got it!" Rory shouted from the next room over. She threw down the book she'd been reading and ran for her door.

We were out of time. Raven hurried to turn on the last electric appliance—but nothing happened.

She dropped her head. "It's not enough."

Something clanged to the ground beside us, and we turned. It was Jack, plugging in the arc welder none of us had known how to use. He cranked the power up all the way, then turned it on.

Suddenly, the power strip sparked. Smoke poured from the electrical outlet, and there was a loud pop as the power went out, plunging both of our rooms into darkness.

"What happened?" one of the Illuminerdy kids yelled. "I can't see."

"Where do I enter the last number?" Rory called.

With the power out, the electric locks in both rooms released. Before the Illuminerdy kids could figure out what had happened, Raven grabbed our door and pulled it open. "We win."

CHAPTER 31
A Fitting Win

Nothing is quite as sweet as celebrating a victory
with your friends and a bag of Halloween
candy fresh from a night of trick-or-treating.

"It's not fair," Dr. Samantha said. "We had the last number."

Raven grinned. "But we opened our door first. And that was the goal."

Principal Redbeard glared, his cheeks as red as the hair covering them. "You cheated."

"No," his grandfather said from where he was sitting in his wheelchair. "They thought outside the box and worked together to accomplish their goal in a way that even I hadn't expected."

He turned to me with a thoughtful expression. "I didn't think you could do it."

I sighed. "Honestly, I wasn't sure we could either. But that's the thing about 'ordinary' kids. Nobody knows what they're capable of until you give them a chance."

Michael held out his hand and flashed me a gapped-tooth grin. "Nice win. But I want a rematch."

I shook my head. "I think I might be done with intelligence tests for a while. For things that are supposed to be about the mind, they're way too hard on my *body*."

We all laughed.

"Does this mean the curse is broken?" Raven asked.

Hubert nodded and held up a shaky hand. "I swear it. And I'm also going to keep my word about not just giving my money to the smartest students."

Principal Redbeard huffed. "I won't take any part in giving money to 'average' children."

"No, you won't," his grandfather said with a devious twinkle in his eye. "In fact, you won't be part of giving money to any children."

"What are you saying?" Principal Redbeard demanded, his lips trembling. "You're not saying you're going to . . ."

The old man nodded. "Your time running the Illuminerdy is done. Perhaps you can get another job as a principal. Or a teacher. Or a custodian. It might teach you the value of hard work and the value of 'ordinary' people."

Jack whispered to Maya.

"Right," she said. "We need to go trick-or-treating. It's almost dark."

Hubert Sullivan smiled. "I hope you get lots of treats. You've earned them."

• • •

"I still can't believe that Mr. Sullivan ruled in our favor," I said as we gathered together on Monday morning. We stood outside the school, comparing the candy we'd gotten trick-or-treating and remembering how angry Principal Redbeard had been when his grandfather ruled us the winners.

"Do you think they'll keep their word?" Maya asked. "Is the Curse of the Illuminerdy broken?"

"I hope so," I said. "At least I haven't had any more stinky pizzas delivered to me yet."

Principal Luna stepped out from the school with a stern expression on her face, her gaze locking on us. "Graysen Foxx, come into my office."

"Uh-oh," Raven said. "Maybe you spoke too soon."

"I'm going to go make sure I don't have any overdue books," Klart said.

Maya and Jack folded their arms. "We'll wait here until you come out."

"Me too," Raven said.

Principal Luna led me into her office and pointed for me to sit down across from her. "I received a number of emails about you today."

"Oh?" I said, my heart skipping like a kid with a new jump rope.

Principal Luna nodded. "It appears that all your overdue books have been returned, your grades are back to normal, your absences have disappeared, and you no longer have any dietary restrictions. Would you like to explain how that is possible?"

I shook my head, feeling as limp as a noddle in a bowl of steaming ramen. "Maybe later. But right now, I think I just want to enjoy not having to eat salt-free crackers and brown bananas for lunch."

"Very well." She clasped her hands together on the desk and frowned. "But there is one other email you *will* need to explain."

"Okay . . ."

"I received a very odd message from a Hubert Sullivan."

I sat back up. "Principal Redbeard's grandfather?"

"You *know* him?"

I gulped. "We've met."

"Then maybe you can explain this." She took a piece of paper out of a drawer, spun it around, and slid it across the desk to me. "It seems that you have been put in charge of distributing an extremely large sum of money."

"What?" I leaned forward to look at the paper and felt my head start to spin. I'd never seen so many zeros in my life.

Principal Luna folded her arms. "I asked our accountant to look into this and it seems to be real. But I don't know how or why. I'd like an explanation."

I pushed up my fedora, unclipped my sticky hand, and set it on the desk. "Well, it all started when Maya and Jack wanted to win the best-decorated classroom contest."

Trying to remember all the details, I told her everything that had happened, starting with finding the medal and

ending with Mr. Sullivan saying that there hadn't been any rule against unlocking the door by blowing the fuse.

By the time I finished, Principal Luna was shaking her head. "So he just gave you control of all this money to—?"

"Donate to schools, and libraries, and scholarships for kids who really need them," I said. "Kids who might not seem super smart at first, but who have a lot to offer if you give them a chance."

Principal Luna blew up her cheeks and released a long, slow breath. "That sounds amazing. But it's a big responsibility."

"I know," I said, wondering how I'd ever be able to do it while still going to school, hanging out with my friends, and hunting for treasure.

"I have an idea," I said after a moment. "You know a lot of people. Do you think you could find some teachers, librarians, and accountants who could handle getting the right money to the right places at the right time? At least until I'm a little older?"

She smiled. "I think I could do that. What would you like to call this organization?"

"I still kind of like *Illuminerdy*," I said. "It has a nice ring to it. But I would like to change the motto."

She raised her eyebrows.

"Instead of *Intelligentia Super Omnia*—intelligence above all," I said, "let's make it *Intelligentia Pro Omnibus*. Intelligence *for* all."

Acknowledgments

Thank you so much to all the people who made this book possible. Thanks to my amazing agent, Michael Bourret, who never tells me any of my ideas are too "out there." Okay, almost never. To my incredible editors, Lisa Mangum and Kristen Evans, who gave me guidance, encouragement, and even some of the best metaphors and similes in this story. And to Troy Butcher and Callie Hansen for giving me so much sales and marketing support, as well as being good friends.

Thanks to Artist Extraordinaire Brandon Dorman, who is a genius at making my ideas come to life.

Thank you, thank you, thank you, to my wife, Jennifer, who after thirty-five years of marriage still laughs at my jokes; my kids, Erica, Scott, Jacob, and Nick; and their spouses, Nick (obviously a different Nick because that would just be way too Luke and Leia), Natalie, Maura, and Isabella, who at least groan at my jokes. And to my grandbabies who aren't babies anymore: Graysen, Lizzy, Jack, Asher, Cameron, Declan, Michael, Joey, and Aurora, who tell me the best jokes.

Acknowledgments

A special thanks to Natalie Savage, who gave me the idea for the music room notation, and to Dave Cebrowski, Andrew Savage, and Michael Young, who helped me polish it.

And a humongous "I wish I was there to thank you in person" THANK YOU to my loyal readers. You are the reason I write. Live the adventure!

Discussion Questions

1. At the beginning of the book, Graysen, Jack, and Maya find the creepy painting for the Halloween contest, but Raven tricks Maya into handing it to her. If you had to decide who got to take the painting to their classroom, who would you give it to? Why do you think they deserved it?

2. In the math room, Raven gets upset with herself when she solves a problem the wrong way. Klart tells her that even though we all make mistakes, it's important to learn from them and try to do better. What have you learned from your mistakes?

3. When Graysen finds the Illuminerdy, he tells them that they should give the prize to his friends as well because they helped solve the puzzles. But Principal Redbeard says that Graysen earned it, since he was the only one who made it to the end of the test. Who do you think is right, and why?

4. The escape room where Graysen, Maya, Jack, Raven, and Klart compete against the Illuminerdy kids has puzzles related to five different subjects—engineering, music,

chemistry, computer programming, and history. If you could pick five puzzle subjects for your own escape room, what would they be?

5. The Illuminerdy believes that their test is the only way of finding kids who can change the world. Do you think someone's true potential can really be measured by a test? Why or why not?

6. Graysen says that even though he and his friends don't have the same training as the Illuminerdy kids, they can solve the puzzles just as fast. How did working together help his group? When have you worked together to solve a problem?

7. As a reward for getting out of the room first, the Illuminerdy lets Graysen decide how to spend their money to help other kids learn and grow. If you were in charge of that money, how would you spend it to help other kids?